KEEPER

OF THE

MIRROR

KEEPER

OF THE

MIrrOR

THE BOOK OF PETER

THERESA NELLIS

atmosphere press

For Mom

—the best unsuspecting sidekick and mirror adjuster around!

For Dad

—my biggest fan who insists I don't sound like a choking chicken when I sing!

For Anjuli

—who would bust out her Tae Kwon Do on those blue-eyed freaks—except for me, *please*!

For My Students

—who were the inspiration for my dark humor—*sorry*!

You Know Who You Are

—thank you for pushing me to be blue instead of *purple*!

Chapter 1

The percussive booming from Peter's heart betrays him, choosing instead to sync with the crying sounds coming from the wooden staircase as she climbs—fast but slow. Warm bile takes pleasure in its slow journey down his throat before laying claim in his stomach.

He whispers, "She's coming!"

Thump! Thump! Thump!

"Quick! Give it to me, Sully. *Please.*"

His knuckles turn white as he tries to extract his sock that's firmly lodged in the dog's mouth like a vice grip.

"Come—on—Sully—LET—GO!"

Thump! Thump! Thump!

"Grrr! You stupid dog! Let—go!"

Thump! Thump! Thump! With each pounding footstep, Peter's coveted iPad clumsily tap dances on top of his tallest dresser.

Meanwhile, Peter throws his body back and digs his

bare feet into the hardwood floor—catching some traction until the dog does the same. A tiny splinter pierces the sensitive flesh of Peter's foot, causing him to look down. The dog continues to pump his body up and down, victoriously yanking the mangled-up sock out of Peter's hands and claiming victory.

Suddenly, the door punches open.

Sully drops the drool-soaked sock hanging from his snaggle-toothed mouth.

"Peter!" screams his mother as spit cascades from her mouth like a tip of a hose. "I told you to get dressed!"

"But—but..."

"Buts are for sitting on! And if you want to ever sit on yours again, you'd better get dressed this instant!"

The door slams shut, sending out a puff of dust.

Peter doesn't hear the crash. Instead, he turns to Sully and says, "What—an—idiot! She doesn't know the difference between but and butts."

The dog resembles a bobble-head doll as he hangs on to Peter's every word.

The door punches open again. "What was that?"

Sully cries out and darts under Peter's bed, causing the bedframe to rattle as the dog's large body attempts to wedge beneath it.

Peter shrugs. "Nothing."

"That's what I thought. Now quit playing with Sully and GET DRESSED! We're late—*again!*"

A string of whimpers echoing out from under the bed replaces the reverberating sound left from her slamming the door. The dog's not-so-attractive rear-end juts out from under the bed—his hind legs waving wildly like an upturned beetle. Chuckling, Peter grabs and misses several times until his hands finally make purchase with Sully's legs.

"Sully," scrunching his face as he tugs, "I'm—totally—embarrassed—for—"

The dog's body loosens and slingshots back at Peter, sending the two flying wildly against the adjacent wall. They hit hard and fall to the floor like deflated balloons. Peter's head rolls to the side, and his eyes widen like saucers. On the hardwood floor, cracked like a spent egg, is his iPad.

"My—my—iPad! She ruins *everything*! You mark my words, Sully," he grits his teeth and says, "I'm—out—of—here!"

Reaching past a neatly folded stack of clean school uniforms, he grabs a crumpled-up one from the floor. Then scoops up the sock he and Sully had fought over. He puts it on. The dog's drool wets each part of his foot until laying claim on his ankle. With his eyes locked on the door, his hands inch closer and closer behind his desk.

Reaching. Reaching.

"Got it!" Like a frog claiming a fly, he grabs a stack of crumpled papers and shoves them into his backpack. Peter drags his feet on the hardwood floor, the wet sock leaving the gooey mark of a snail as he heads downstairs and towards the door.

Stretching her neck out from the smokestack coming from a pan on top of the stove, Mrs. Powell says, "You can't leave yet. You haven't had any breakfast. I made you pancakes."

"No," Peter snickers, "you just *burnt* pancakes. There's not a chance of me eating—well, of eating *that*." Reaching out, he scratches Sully between the ears and says, "I'll *smell ya* later!"

Peter rights his upturned sneakers beside the door and forces his feet into them. The laces trail behind like the tentacles of a jellyfish. Sully jumps up and grabs at them, sending Peter crashing backward onto the unforgiving black and white tiled kitchen floor.

Crash!

"Ugh! My back. Am I—am I dead?"

"No, Peter. You are very much alive." She lets out a long sigh. "Trust me."

Like a popping pimple, papers push out from his unzipped backpack. Reaching her hands out towards them, she asks, "Hey, what's this?"

"Oh, ugh. It's nothing."

He jumps up, quickly snatches the papers, and pulls open the heavy kitchen door. The weatherstripping makes a soft *whoosh* as it smacks off the century-old doorframe. He takes a few steps and kicks his mother's favorite yellow rose bush, sending petals fluttering to the ground like the delicate wings of a butterfly.

Skipping down the driveway, he skids and comes to a complete halt. The nosy neighbor and her prissy little dog, Miss Darcy, stand at the edge of his driveway. Her timing isn't coincidental. And that dog is only for show—both with its pompous appearance and the opportunity it provides her to spy on the Powells, especially Peter. The nosy old woman had been in the neighborhood for ages. She was even the God Mother to his late aunt. But as his mother tells it, something had changed when they returned to the family home. Despite his nagging, his mother would never tell him *what had changed and why*.

Now, the nosy neighbor clutches her oversize handbag

against her chest with one arm and pulls back the yappy dog donning a bedazzled pink collar and matching lace dress with her other.

She screams at Peter, "Stop looking at Miss Darcy! You might—might change her or something!" Bending down and talking to the dog, "Don't worry about that boy, pumpkin. You can do a nice little potty right here in their yard. Maybe even on that hideous rose bush. That's a horrible place to put it anyway. Besides, everyone knows those aren't the type of roses you plant in New York. They'll be good as dead by winter. You'd be doing them a favor."

The nosy neighbor's long slip drops below her dress as she stands up. Her white orthopedic shoes with Velcro straps add an extra inch or two to her already challenged stature. All the while, her intense gaze never once leaving Peter.

"Miss Darcy," she says with a low growl, "You mark my words—there's something not right with that boy. He's just like that—*that man*—if you can even call him that."

Peter cries out, "You know, I'm right here. What do you even mean? Who? My dad? I'm nothing like him. But I get you don't think he's a man—he's more of a—"

"I owe you no explanation, child." Lowering her voice and thumbing her chest, "But—I—know. I know it all. I know that you—"

She turns her gaze to the sound of the next-door neighbors spilling out of their house. Peter winces as the door closes and opens. Again and again. Couldn't they all leave at the same blasted time? It's like watching *The Old Woman and the Shoe* sending her kids off to school.

The nosy neighbor turns to Miss Darcy. "Come on,

honey bear. We've stayed here too long already. Let's go."

Peter cries out, "Wait! What is it that you know? *Please, just tell me!*"

As she ambles out of sight, he drops his head and absently kicks a small rock on the sidewalk. The school is only a few blocks away—one of the benefits of living in a small, upstate New York community. Just about everything is within walking distance. In just a few short minutes, he's already at the school marquee announcing the upcoming *Bring Your Own Device To School Night*. Like he'd ever willingly go back to school when he didn't have to.

Peter passes by the school's overzealous traffic guard standing at full attention as the unofficial gatekeeper. Except, there isn't a gate—he isn't guarding anything—and he's an 85-year-old retired volunteer and *not* a traffic guard at all.

Seeing Peter, the man takes an exaggerated deep breath and stands at his full stature of four foot nothing, complete with pants hiked up to his armpits. And just in case his pants might slide down to his waist, red suspenders are firmly in place to take over the job. The man rolls his eyes like a sick hyena and motions for Peter to come closer. Peter reaches down and pinches behind his knee, piercing the tender skin with his nails and bringing a pained look to his face.

Mr. Johnson raises his black, bushy unibrow. It's hard to tell which hair is longer, his unkept unibrow or his protruding nasal hair with wet snot dangling from the tips. He tilts his head closer to Peter, and he can see a large clump of brown earwax making itself right at home in one of the man's large, floppy ears.

Peter quivers his lower lip and cries out, "I'm—I'm—late—because," sniffling hard, "because—of—*her*—again!"

Peter winces as Mr. Johnson pats his back. The sweat from the man's damp hand soaks through Peter's shirt.

"There, there, Peter. You go on inside now and try to have yourself a good day."

"Yes, sir."

Calling out to him, "Hey, have you had breakfast today?"

"No, sir."

"You WHAT? How are you supposed to feed that brain of yours without any breakfast?"

"I'll—I'll be okay," he says, dropping his head and studying his soggy sock.

"Nonsense." The old man lifts the radio attached to his belt and pushes the button. "Gate 1 to Base. Gate 1 to Base."

"Go ahead, Mr. Johnson," cries back Mrs. Campbell, the school secretary.

"Peter's late for school again, and he hasn't had breakfast. Do you happen to have—?"

"Say no more," she says into the radio. Releasing the button, she says, "because I can't stand it if you do." Pushing the button again, "I have a box of those cereal bars he likes. Send him in."

Mr. Johnson reaches his sweaty palm out again and pats Peter's arm. "Now you go on into the office. Mrs. Campbell will see to it that you aren't hungry."

Peter turns and muffles a dramatic dry heave into his elbow, then forces his lips to part open like the Cheshire Cat. "Thanks, Mr. Johnson. I don't know what I'd do without you."

Peter winks at the reflection cast back at him as he

pulls open the front door to Crossroads Middle School. In stark contrast to his parents' neatly coiffed chocolate brown hair, he has tousled blond hair, wrinkled clothes, and smells of mildew and dirty feet. His dark brown eyes contrast sharply with his overall appearance of a pale, limp noodle. His bizarre ears round off his overall odd appearance. It looks like someone played Mr. Potato Head with his body parts and attached all the wrong sizes and color features.

Mrs. Campbell looks up when she hears Peter walk into the office. "You poor child," she says, holding up one of his favorite candy bars masquerading as a cereal bar—a brand his mother only buys for an occasional treat.

He eagerly snatches it and unwraps it in one fluid motion. But just like those pesky wait staff at restaurants, Principal Payne walks in just as he shoves half the bar into his mouth.

Mrs. Payne says, "Hello, Peter. I see it's another day without any breakfast."

He looks at her and shrugs.

"Do you have your homework today?"

Chomp, chomp. "I needed help with it." *Chomp, chomp.* "But my mom," he says as he pushes his eyebrows together, "was at the beauty shop getting her hair and nails done."

"I—see. Did you ask your *father* for help then?"

"She makes him go to work early and stay late." *Sniffle.* "I'm *always* alone."

Tilting her head to the side, "Really?"

"Yes, and she spends all of our money. That's why I don't have enough school uniforms." And with the savagery of Sully sniffing a pile of dog poop, he throws up his arms and breathes in the smell of his armpits. "Hey, do you think I smell?"

"Um. Well. I think." Regrouping, she says, "Well, I'm going to check this out. I—umm—have to do something. You just go on to class before you miss much more."

"Yes, ma'am."

Chapter 2

Peter struts home from school with earbuds sticking out of his long ears. Years ago, his father had grabbed ahold of their pointy tips and said that one day the rest of his body would catch up to their size—which sent his mother into a fit of hysteria. His father never spoke of it again.

Now, he bellows out the lyrics to his favorite hip-hop song at the top of his lungs as he opens the kitchen door—sounding more like a choking chicken than a 13-year-old boy. Pulling off his backpack, he dropkicks it evenly between two colored tiles.

"Bummer! I was trying for an all-white tile today."

Opening the refrigerator door, he smirks and grabs his father's coveted pastrami on rye sandwich and darts off to his bedroom—lest his father attempts to greet him or to ask him any annoying questions. *Like...*

"Did anything special happen today?"

"What did you learn?"

"Do you have any homework?"

"Did you make any friends?"

Blah, blah, blah!

Sully had opened one eye at the sound of the door opening and closing. Waiting until Peter made for the stairs, he emerges from his slumber, lets out a playful bark, and chases after him—fast on his heels. He grabs at Peter's stinky feet and manages to drag off one of the socks from earlier that morning.

DSSH! Peter goes down hard and smacks his hands and knees off the wood stairs. He gets up and keeps running to his room—still trying to avoid his father. Peter smugly laughs at the dog as the safety of his bedroom door quickly approaches. Once Peter was too slow and Sully had pounced on his back and refused to get off until he had called for his father. Once he freed Peter, the barrage of school-related questions followed.

Now, throwing open his door, he screams and sends the sandwich hurling against the wall. It falls to the floor. Pastrami shoots out from the folds of the wax paper. Sully drops the now mushy sock proudly hanging from his snaggle-toothed mouth like a fresh kill. His four legs fly in every direction as he tries to stop on the slippery, polished wood floor. The dog smacks into the adjacent wall and falls to the ground like a squished spider.

"Dad, come quick! We were—we were robbed!"

Crickets.

Taking the steps two at a time, screaming all the while, "Dad—dad, everything's missing from my room!" Flailing his arms up and down like one of those inflatable air dancers parked outside a car dealership, he screams, "It's all—it's all—GONE! What—what happened?"

His father swallows hard, then adjusts his newspaper

with a well-rehearsed snapping of its pages. And sighs.

"Dad! Dad!"

His eyes continue to fix on the newspaper.

"Hey, dad! What—what happened?"

Smacking his lips together, Mr. Powell says, "Hey—Peter—pass me the salt."

"What? That makes no sense. What does that even mean?" he sputters out. "Is anything of yours missing, too?"

Again, not looking up, he releases another long sigh. "No—it ALL seems to be here, including *you*."

"Look at me! Don't you even care my stuff is gone?"

"Nailed it! Your principal called—*again*."

Like an instant facelift, Peter's furrowed browline perks up. He chuckles. "Oh yeah! Um—what did she want this time?"

Exasperation chokes out his father's disinterest. He squeals, *"This time! This time!"*

Rolling his eyes, Peter says, "How perceptive of you. Yes, *this* time."

"Your principal reported us."

"What, like you have to write a report or something? If you want extra work, I'll give you some of mine. Try to pretend like it's my handwriting. Mrs. Kunkel figured it out last time."

"No! A report to people who are going to investigate us for being bad parents!"

"Well, maybe you should try harder. Truth hurts."

"Oh yeah, you know what else hurts!"

Expecting it, Peter ducks as the newspaper whooshes past his nose.

"Well, after today, no, Peter. I—simply—don't—care."

"That's because nobody wants any of your STUPID STUFF! That's why it's all still here, and mine's gone!"

Right on cue, his father's pupils flare. A devilish look appears on his face. "So, I guess you've gotten yourself a job now—have you?"

Throwing a provocative eyebrow up, he pauses. Then dramatically cups his hand to his ear. "What's that? Right. No—no, you haven't. Well then—news flash—kid! NOTHING here belongs to you! So yeah— someone does want *our things* since we're the ones with jobs, and it all belongs to ME AND YOUR MOTHER! You have no idea what we've sacrificed for you."

"Oh, yeah? What exactly did *you* sacrifice, old man?"

"More than you know."

"Enlighten me, Tom. No. On second thought, don't bother." Throwing his arms up and screaming like a jackal, he pauses and turns his head upward like a lion detecting its prey. In other words, he hears his mother's car pull into the driveway. He turns back to his father, "You're useless! I'll get it straight from the horse's mouth!"

Peter whips open the kitchen door with such force that it bounces off the doorstop and slams shut. Running towards the car like a linebacker, he rips open the driver's side door. Panting hard and fast, he fixes his mother with a murderous stare.

"Well, thank you, Peter. I must say, I don't think you've ever opened the door for me before—even when I'm walking right behind you. You usually play the *hurry up and get through the door before it hits you in the head game*. It looks like there's some hope for you after all."

"Not a chance. Hey, where's my stuff? Were we robbed or something? YOUR husband is completely useless."

"MY husband—hmm—not YOUR father? Okay, then." Shaking her head and grinning, revealing those tiny little wrinkles beside her fierce brown eyes. "No, Peter, we weren't robbed. I gave it away. Every—last—bit—of—it."

"Now why would you do a stupid thing like that?"

"Why? Why?" sending her voice several uncomfortable octaves higher. "You dare to ask why?"

Upturning his hands, he asks, "Um, isn't that what I just said?"

"And there it is, folks!" she theatrically says as she throws her hands into the air. "Peter Jonathan Powell wants to know why! Well, let's start with the fact that I made you pancakes for breakfast."

"Correction," he says, throwing up one finger. "You burnt pancakes for breakfast."

"Your principal accused us of not feeding you. And you have a dozen clean and pressed school uniforms. She said you asked her if you smell!"

Half of his mouth turns upward, "Yeah, I was going for the eau-de-toilet vibe."

"Now people are going to come here and ask about our family. They've already started talking to the neighbors."

"Oh yeah? Well, did they talk to the nosy neighbor yet? I'm sure she'll give them an earful. Well," he says as he throws his bottom lip out, "you'd better put all my things back this instant. I'd hate to tell those people that you *deprive me of anything else.*"

"Well, if you're going to make up lies, it's better to have something to talk about that's *actually* true!"

"Oh, yeah? Well, you just wait and see!"

Peter slams her door shut.

"Oh, thank you."

"I—I didn't mean to." He whips around and stomps his feet, pausing at the back door.

"Great—now what? SHE'S outside, and HE'S inside."

He turns and kicks the yellow rose bush and sulks towards the rusty old shed that sits off to the side of the house. Cupping his hands, he looks through the yellow-tinted window. The sight of an intricate spider web littering the space just beyond the window sends goosebumps cascading down his arms. Looking over his shoulder, he pushes open the creaky door that belongs in a haunted house. One of the rusted hinges from the door frame snaps off, and the door starts to fall on him. Breathing in fast, he slams his body against the door and forces it shut.

Throwing his hands to his hips, he says, *"Now that was smart!"* As he looks around, something shimmers off to the side catches his eye. It's hidden behind a tower of old boxes stacked from floor to ceiling. Hadn't he been here dozens of times before? Something seemed out of place. Something hidden. But he had seen it. Or maybe he felt it. No. That was just crazy. His tongue flops out of his mouth and off to the side as he surveys the boxes and finds a small open space. Bringing his hands together like a swimmer diving into a pool, he pushes the boxes aside, revealing a peculiar-looking mirror.

A thick layer of cobwebs adorns the old mirror like an old woman wearing a shawl. He pushes his fingertips in further and rubs the mirror's dulled surface, removing a layer of dust that settles between his fingers that now resemble the webbed duck feet. Pushing in still deeper, he pulls apart the boxes and sends them toppling over like falling dominos. The dust darkens the air around him, and he begins having a fit of sneezes. Ogre sounding sneezes. Ones that are strong enough to clear your nasal passages in a single pass.

Once the dust settles, the full mirror comes into view. It stands at about five feet tall and is weathered and scratched. It has an intricate design of ornate serpents carved around it, making it nearly impossible to see where one snake ends and the other begins. He rubs his hand over a two-headed serpent with a double-forked, red tongue. Rubbing his pointer finger down the length of the mirror, he pulls off another thick layer of dust. The color drains from his face as he examines the dust, letting out a soft, shaky gasp. Wincing like he's walking on a herd of sea urchins with their long spines stabbing into his sensitive flesh.

He brings his fingers to his nose and sniffs deeply, casting an upwards glance and leaving behind a thin coating of dust on his nostrils. His nose aches and twitches with a mind of its own. Suddenly, he lets out another thunderous sneeze like a blowhorn. The force manages to remove most of the dust taking up residence inside his nostrils, but not the brown soot-looking layer that's now covering his entire face.

"Well now, what do we have here? And why do I get the feeling that I—WASN'T—supposed to—see—this?"

Chapter 3

Peter paces a mere five steps from one side of his room to the other. *"Seriously! Those people have the combined IQ of peanut if they expect me to rot inside this wasteland of a bedroom."*

He opens the door and bellows at the top of his lungs, "Hey, I think I just saw a team of tumbleweeds going past my room!"

His mother screams back, "That's great! Let us know if you see a roadrunner!"

Chuckling, his father yells, "Beep beep! Or the Acme truck. Better yet, let us know if an anvil falls from your ceiling!"

Peter yells back, "That's just stupid. Anvils don't fall from ceilings! And what is an Acme truck? Are you making fun of my acne or something?"

Chuckling louder, Mr. Powell turns to his wife and says, "That child has no idea what we're talking about."

She replies, "It's *only* the best cartoon ever."

Peter slams his door and scampers like a vermin to the

only other thing in his bedroom besides his bed—his desk. He opens the top right drawer. Like the opening of a jack-in-the-box, it spews out random papers and homework assignments. Immersing both hands deep inside its crevices, he tosses everything over his shoulder and onto the floor until finding a notepad and pencil.

Cackling to himself, *"But what to do?"*

He alternates between tapping the pencil tip to the notepad and then to his chin and titles his list, *Top 10 Ways to Completely Break My Parents.*

"Narrowing this down to only ten ideas is going to be tough. I have so—many—options. But, I don't want to give myself carpal tunnel syndrome by writing too much. Tsk, tsk! Haven't I taught those people anything by now?"

His father should have known better than to taunt him earlier. He made that stupid comment that he had a job and Peter didn't.

"Well, that could easily be remedied. And what if *he* didn't have a job either? Oh, the jabs I could give that man. *Hey—Dad, don't think you're going to share my cardboard box when we get kicked out of our house because YOU don't have a job either. Or—I guess you can't pretend to have early morning meetings anymore to avoid taking me to school. Or—does this mean that Mom wears the pants in the family now?"*

He's in eighth grade with that people-pleasing, Buck-Toothed Buckley. The boy's front teeth rival those of a beaver. His parents must have been psychic when they named him. And all Peter would have to do is talk to Buck-Tooth. A most intriguing story would be all that's necessary—a most fanciful story—one worthy of canning his father *right—on—the—spot*. Who cares that it would all be a lie. And Buck-Tooth is gullible enough to believe anything Peter says. Once Peter watched Buck-Tooth swallow a watermelon seed in kindergarten, and he told him that he'd grow a watermelon in his stomach. Peter then pointed to the fat cafeteria lady and said he'd watched her eating watermelon that very morning. Buck-Tooth was so upset that he wouldn't leave the restroom until he heaved up his entire lunch.

But now, figuring out a way to watch the entire thing would take even more planning and plotting than the whole act itself. And if he could get it on video, he could hold it over their heads forever. He could even put it on social media, and it would surely go viral. He'd be famous. A bone-chilling cackle cuts through his bedroom door.

His tongue flops out of his mouth as he absentmindedly licks the skin just below his bottom lip. It's been a bad habit of his for as long as he could remember. And since he schemes so often, the skin around his mouth looks like a permanently painted circus clown.

"And what was I thinking? It would be *bad form* to leave Kate out of the plan. Rude even."

A wicked smile pokes through his frown like the sun peeking out on a cloudy day, at odds with the severe pointing of his eyebrows. Low and fierce growls from Sully interrupt Peter, causing his tongue to reflexively finds its way back into his mouth. Lifting his shoulder, he turns his head and wipes the drool onto a clean school shirt. Now flopping his tongue to the other side, he returns to his evil plotting, not even looking to see why Sully's blood is boiling over with rage. In Peter's defense, the dog is notorious for barking at the feral cats that nonchalantly parade around the house's perimeter with their fluffy tails waving to and fro.

Sully could often be seen dragging Peter halfway down Crestfallen Court in hot pursuit of one of the adversarial felines. On one occasion, Sully went around a telephone pole while being walked on a leash—followed by Peter—then Sully going even faster—then Peter trying still harder to catch him with his skinny little chicken legs. Then...BAM! There's Peter and Sully wrapped tightly around the pole by the dog leash. Judging by the bewildered look on the dog's face at the time, Sully didn't realize until it was too late that the cat had outsmarted him. It's been game-on for the dog ever since.

To add insult to injury, the tutu-donning dog next door peed on Peter's foot as she went by. And that nosey neighbor saw everything and just left him there, mumbling something that sounded like a prayer and making the cross symbol over her forehead as she passed by. He made it a point to throw eggs at her house that Halloween and again on Thanksgiving for good measure.

His temples begin to pulsate and throb with increased vigor. He laughs and shrugs. *"Some people exercise; I plan malevolent acts. To each their own."*

He grits his teeth and says, "Put—a—sock—in—it—Sully! I'm plotting my most wicked revenge yet." Chuckling, "Now that's saying a lot—even for ME!"

His parents liked to say he gave them a gray hair for every mean thing he did to them. *"That's so rude!"* Judging by this standard, they should both be entirely gray by now. Extra points for premature hair loss! *"After all, I simply hate to be short-changed!"*

He fitfully pounds on his window to scare the cats off without even looking up, but Sully continues to growl anyway. After it's clear the dog isn't going to stop, Peter squishes his face and turns towards the window. There's no prancing tabby cat outside. No lasagna-eating orange cat. No ragamuffin or ragdoll cats. Instead, the dog's attention is gripped by something else outside. *But what?*

Turning back towards the dog, "Well, since you won't stop bugging me, let's go see what's out there."

Sully jumps up and follows Peter outside. The two exit through the kitchen door that leads outside. They pass the rosebush. Peter gives it a swift kick and sends some more yellow petals flying all about. Sully runs up ahead, turns around, then lifts his leg and pees on the rosebush.

"Ten points for Sully!" screams Peter. "Now, when you're done clowning around, mind showing me what's wrong?"

Sully's head again resembles a bobblehead doll. Then as if remembering why they were out there, he runs towards the rusty old shed. Throwing his front paws up on the door and looking through the window, he lets out an intimidating growl. The yellow tint of the windowpane darkens with the dog's hot breath.

"What? The shed? Oh, that's right. I found something in there today."

Peter puts one hand on the knob and the other higher up on the door to support it.

"Watch out, Sully. This thing's busted." But the dog doesn't move. The door creaks as Peter pulls on it. Despite his attempts at securing it, it still begins to fall. He throws his body against it, but it's too late. It falls to the ground like a cut tree, leaving a bare doorframe. Sully pushes past Peter and darts into the shed. He runs to the space between the boxes and stops right in front of the mirror.

He growls and bares his teeth.

Chuckling, "Are you afraid of your reflection, too, silly old boy? I've heard the same thing about me a time or two. My stupid parents and their *per—fect* appearances and all. Then there's ME! It's tough pulling off such a sloppy image. You can't just roll out of bed and look like this," he says, motioning towards himself from head to toe. "It took me years to sculpt and cultivate this image."

The hair on Sully's black and brown-furred back is standing up on end like the quills of a porcupine. Peter walks towards him with his hand outstretched.

"Sully, get over...!"

But before Peter can even finish, the dog leaps directly at the mirror with his muscular back legs flexing as he propels his front legs forward, his sharp teeth menacing and at the ready. Peter grimaces, crouches down a bit, closes one eye, and expects the whole thing to topple over and shatter—wanting to see the impending chaos of the smashing mirror and his ability to claim innocence for once. But it doesn't. Instead, there's a loud humming sound like a bug getting sizzled by a bug zapper. Then there's a brilliant flash of white light like a solar flare causing Peter's eyes to water. He winces and looks away. When he looks back, Sully wasn't there. He had vanished right inside the mirror! Buzz! Thuwp! Flash! Gone, dog!

"WHOA! How—did—you—do—that? Hey—I want to have a go at it!"

Peter pats his hands all over the reflective surface of the mirror. He slides his hands along the outside frame, feeling every crack and crevice. A small splinter embeds itself into his finger, causing a tiny droplet of crimson blood to fall to the floor. He steps one foot at a time onto the legs at the base of the mirror. Once the frame is supporting his entire body weight, he does a little bounce. The mirror lets out a moan. Nothing.

This time watching for fractures in the wood, he slides his fingers along each serpent, spending extra time on the ones with bared fangs. Still nothing.

Using the palm of his hand, he feels the mirror's reflective surface again, chuckling as he leaves his greasy handprints behind on the glass. He sticks his tongue out, pauses for a moment, and licks the mirror lengthwise, removing a layer of dust and leaving more snail-like film behind. He coughs for several seconds.

"Furball!"

Grasping the mirror, he swivels it up—down—side to side. *WHOOSH! WHOOSH!* There's a sound emanating from it, much like his *old* lightsaber. Old because his mother got rid of nearly everything in his room. The hair on his arms stands up tall.

"Weird! Must be static electricity or something."

Whispering to himself, *"I know you're there, Tom and Kate! Are you mad that I broke the door? You're not fooling me for a..."*

He slaps his hand over his mouth and tiptoes over to the open door space. He pops his head out fast and looks around. His eyes drop—no parents.

Rubbing down the blond hair on his arms, he says, *"Okay—okay, then. Where is it? Where's the camera? Or is it a projector? Is there a secret trap door? Perhaps it's a hologram, and it wasn't Sully going through the mirror at all."*

He uses a deep and exaggerated tone as he motions his arms like he's waving a magic wand and says, *"Mirror, reveal your secrets! No, then? Okay, how about abracadabra! Kalamazoo—I hate you."*

Pulling back his leg, he kicks the mirror and releases a small crack along the base. A charlie horse grips his calf, and he lets out a cry. Giving up, he returns to his bedroom. The clock circles the 12 several times. He twiddles his thumbs and then rubs a few handprints onto his bedroom window. He opens his mouth and breathes his hot breath onto the cool windowpane, and writes, *"PARENTS FOR SALE: BUY ONE, GET ONE FREE!"*

He flops onto his bed and theatrically throws his arms out on either side of him. He looks up at the ceiling and tilts his head as he studies an oblong-type shape with streaks running through it like a haphazard stream running down a mountainside. The center is dark, and it lightens towards the outer edges. His eyes begin to flutter and get heavy until he finally dozes off.

A warm pool of drool on his face awakens him with a start. He grabs another clean school uniform and dries his face with it. Balling it up, he throws it on the floor, joining the contents of his desk drawer. It's dark outside now.

"Sully! Sully come here!" he calls out.

He has never slept a night without him. Peter doesn't have any friends because he's not interested in *being a friend*, so sleepovers are a non-issue. He didn't have any extended family to speak of, which made holiday get-togethers the same old boring people as usual: just the three of them. The two people responsible for bringing his aggravating mother into this world had died before he was even born. His mother had a sister, but she won't ever talk about her other than the fact that she died, too. His dead aunt probably hated her just as much as he does.

On the issue of his paternal grandparents—who were they? They live on the other side of the country but never visit. He's not even sure if he knows what they look like. What's peculiar is that he often hears his father talking about how close they had been at one point. Maybe they didn't like who he married. He could most definitely understand that.

Peter fell asleep and managed to contort himself like a Bavarian pretzel. The soreness, coupled with his flair for the dramatics, looks pathetically like a giraffe learning how to walk for the very first time. He fumbles around the house, hitting everything in his path, not bothering to pick up what he knocks over.

Crash! A fancy glass vase with a dozen long-stemmed yellow roses smashes to the floor. He makes an exception and stops to pick up the roses. He smells their beautiful fragrance and then pops their heads off one by one—then grinds them with his foot into the white shag carpet in the living room. A thorn catches his barefoot, and he wipes the crimson liquid onto the rug, careful to avoid another thorn.

"Okay, dumb dog, what are you up to? I hope you tore open the kitchen garbage trying to get to last night's dinner." At the mention of food, Peter's stomach lets out a loud growl. "I hope you gave THEM a tough time!" Letting out a chuckle, he asks, "I wonder, did the student finally surpass the teacher? On second thought, there's no chance of that."

His futile search for the spirited dog continues until there's only one room left—his parents' bedroom. He assumes a secret ninja position and cracks the door open, careful to avoid the dip in the floor that would creak and reveal him. Peering in, he drops his mouth. His parents are sound asleep in their mahogany sleigh bed. And no bouncing dog is waiting to prance on him.

Squinting his eyes and tensing up, anger grips him at the thought of them feigning sleep. He grabs the glass of ice-cold water on the nightstand beside his father. Without hesitation, he launches the water directly at them, sending an ice cube bouncing g off his father's forehead.

His parents wake with a start and let out screams that could shatter glass. Rubbing his forehead, Mr. Powell repugnantly says Peter's name through gritted teeth and surveys the water all over their soft blue linen blankets.

"Okay—okay, I get it! You had your fun with me. You're mad at me. NOW—GET—OVER—IT—TOM—AND—KATE! I want my dog back NOW so I can go to sleep! Do you hear me!" he screams. Droplets of hot spittle savagely shoot out in every direction from his mouth.

Shaking his head, he turns to his wife and mutters, "He's gone to the dark side. I told you he would."

"I was so afraid of that. Oh, Tom, I hoped it would skip a generation."

"No, dear. I think that's male pattern baldness."

Peter stares blankly at them.

"Honey," says Mr. Powell, "I think..."

Peter screams, "Who cares what you think! Am I going to go bald?"

Mrs. Powell grits her teeth and smiles without those tiny lines framing her soft brown eyes. "Yup! Just like a cue ball."

Peter's narrowed eyes widen. He feverishly paces back and forth and runs his hands through his messy blond hair. Sweat forms above his brows as he starts to feel his heart beating in his throat. *Baboom, baboom, baboom!*

Mrs. Powell orders, "Peter Jonathan Powell, go—to—bed!"

"So...if you didn't do it..."

Mr. Powell smacks his tongue off the roof of his mouth several times. "And what did we do this time? Breathe perhaps?"

"That goes without saying. But Sully needs our help," Peter says with tears in his eyes.

Mrs. Powell sits up straight. "What happened to him?"

"Sully went *through* that stupid mirror that YOU put in the shed! Now YOU have to help me! This is all your fault! I'm warning you now—HELP ME OR ELSE!"

Mrs. Powell's face upturns, and she says, "But how did you even find that? No, that's just not possible."

Peter yells, "Oh, yeah! Well—it—did!"

Mrs. Powell turns to her husband and whispers under her breath, "Do you think?"

Mr. Powell answers, "I don't know. Do you?"

"It can't be. No, definitely not. Only *they* can."

Seething with anger, they turn to Peter and yell in unison, "GET—OUT—NOW!"

"See—this is exactly why I HATE YOU BOTH! Nobody—else—likes—you—two—EITHER, Tom and Kate! That's why you don't have any friends!"

His father scoffs, "Well, well! Isn't that the pot calling the kettle black!"

"That's a stupid saying. Pots come in all sorts of colors," screams Peter. "You're so dumb!"

His mother's eyes bulge like someone is choking her. She shouts at the top of her lungs, "We don't have any friends because you chase them all off! Do you remember the Graysons?" Now lowering her voice in striking clarity, "You put a frog in Mrs. Grayson's brand-new Coach purse. It cost me a week's pay just to replace it!"

Chuckling, "Yeah, that was a good one. It took me a long time to find that frog, too. Talk about perseverance!"

"And then there's Mr. Grayson. You heard him say his blueprints were the only copies he had of that project he spent months working on. One that would have put food on his family's table. Then *mysteriously,* the pages were superglued together!"

"You know, I didn't escape unscathed from that one. I got superglue on my fingers and couldn't play video games for two whole days until it wore away!"

"And then their sweet twin daughters, Sadie and Sophie. You snuck into their rooms, read their diaries, and told everyone at school what they said. The girls were so humiliated that they had to switch schools in the middle of the school year!"

"Geez, you always say you want me to do more reading. Besides, it was a special service to the school. I should get an award or something. It helped to lower the student to teacher ratio."

Peter's father stands up to his full stature, comically offset by his flannel pajamas. "Peter..."

"Now will you look at that," Peter snickers, "I forgot how tall you are because you're usually on your butt! Save it, Tom; I'm out of here!"

He slams the door with a loud THUD, sending a framed picture of two teenage girls smashing to the floor. The girls in the picture were carefree. One had an arm draped around the other as they stood in front of a split-rail fence. One had long brown hair with chocolate brown eyes. The other had long, wavy blonde hair with matching chocolate brown eyes. Shards of glass splinter off in every direction.

His mother screams, "NO," in what feels like slow motion as she lunges towards the direction of the falling picture. Her arms outstretched as she falls to the ground. Her elbows hit hard as she skids across the carpet, leaving deep friction burns. "Oh no! That's... that's...that's..."

Peter hears her cry out from the other side of the door. He thrusts it open and mocks, "Quit stu-stu-stuttering and finally tell me who that other dumb woman is in the picture besides YOU!"

His parents turn and look at each other. The blood rushes to Mr. Powell's face and he turns away. Mrs. Powell hangs her head low.

"Yeah! I didn't think so!"

He stomps back to his bedroom and punches the freshly painted wall as he goes. The label on the can of paint said the color was "*Sea Salt*," but it just looks like blue and green vomited on each other. His puny fist leaves nothing more than a tiny little pinprick—barely even visible.

Chapter 4

Peter's parents had recently remodeled his bedroom first before setting off to update their own. They outfitted his bedroom with a stunning oak bed with a built-in trundle and matching desk. To his liking, Peter spends most of his time either in his bedroom, the bathroom, or the kitchen. He tries to avoid his parents at every turn, but a kid must eat—and eat often.

The kitchen pantry has markings of Peter's growth that his mother insists upon making every year on his birthday before he's allowed to open his gifts. Pressing a ruler to the backside of his head, she painstakingly forces him to stand against the wall to chart his growth, which she had done for 13 consecutive years. When she wasn't looking, he had tried to erase the lines, but the indentation of where she had pushed down hard with the pencil remained despite his best attempts to irradicate them.

Now, he rests his forehead on the cool windowpane in his bedroom. His deep breaths cause his four-times-replaced double window to fog up. The first replacement was for practical reasons—the original windows were drafty.

The second time was when he threw his video game remote control so hard that it put a small chip in the window and quickly spread, causing it to shatter like a spider's web.

The third time was when he was exceedingly annoyed at being told to close the window because the heat was on. So, he slammed it shut, and it cracked like an egg.

The fourth time he used his markers and sketched a dartboard on his window, then used metal-tipped darts and put lots of tiny holes in the glass until the spider came back to visit. *Snap, crackle, pop!*

Droplets of sweat now fall from his forehead and form a small pool on the refinished wooden floor. *"Think, Peter, think! Okay, Sully had just lunged at the mirror, and voila...he went right into it like a veritable black hole. If I charge right at it, I should just go through it, too. Right? But what if it only works for dogs? What if I cut my handsome face? I would walk around looking like a monster for the rest of my life! Well, I could just get another dog. Ugh, but then I'd have to potty train it! Um— yeah—okay! I—can—do—this!"*

He jumps up and awkwardly places one wobbling leg in front of the other—starts—stops—begins again—and stops again. He waits. Motionless. Almost catatonic. Taking another slow and deep breath, then letting out a laugh.

"Okay, Peter, get a grip."

He starts moving again. His expensive, once white tennis shoes squeak on the sweat-drenched floor. It sounds like a herd of middle schoolers descending the stairs after the rain. The squeaking sound of sneakers never gets old!

Peter opens the kitchen door. Slams it. Opens it again. And slams it again. He shoots his leg out to the side and kicks more petals off the yellow rose bush on his way to the shed. Shuttering, he steps on the shed door and looks up.

"I'm outta here if a creepy spider crawls on me!"

He walks up to the mirror. As if in a challenge, he throws his hands up and emits a serpent-like hiss, sending spittle cascading from his mouth. He winces and tucks his head down so his chin is nestled lightly on his bony chest. Pushing off on his legs, he stops his momentum by theatrically throwing himself to the floor—hitting with a loud thud and knocking the wind out of him.

"UH!"

He pulls himself up onto all fours with the speed of a three-toed sloth, then slowly stands. The first thing he spies is his father's expensive new chainsaw and throws it to the ground like a stone, popping the chain off with his foot. He fitfully darts his head back and forth. After several minutes, he lets out a wicked smile and grabs what he wanted.

Standing in front of the mirror again, he smartly puts on a black bicycle helmet with Mohawk-style hair streaming out in blond spikes from the center. He tucks his head down, shakes his head back and forth as he tries not to think any more about the impending insanity. Holding his breath, he plows head-first at the scratched-up old mirror with the entire force and speed of his skinny body.

The last thing he sees is his distorted image that looks

like the reflection from a funhouse mirror, and then—just like with Sully—there's a blinding bright flash of light. *WHOOSH!* With his very next breath, he's standing on the other side of the old mirror. Breathing deeply, he throws up both hands and wiggles his fingers. His mouth counts off 1, 2, 3, 4, 5, 6, 7, 8, 9, 10.

"Phew, still 10!"

He lifts his arms and shakes them, then does the same with his legs. He does what *he* might consider a dance, but others might be inclined to describe it as a chicken pecking at food complete with spindly legs and a wobbly neck. He turns around and looks at the shed through the other side of the mirror.

"Creepy!"

His hot, fast breath causes condensation to form on the mirror. *"Just in case you can see this, Tom and Kate,"* he says as he runs his finger down the length of the mirror. Without hesitation, he writes I—HATE—YOU! He quickly erases it. He breathes on the mirror again, then writes his message backward so they can correctly read it. *Now, who said he didn't have manners?*

He looks around and lets out a soft gasp. Standing inside an eerie cave, he can see several torches scattered around, supplying only a modest amount of light, playing fanciful games with his shadow as he walks. Sometimes he looks tall and thin, then short and fat. The shadows cast from the spikes on his helmet elongate his appearance like a medieval-era knight of the roundtable. He puffs his chest, unfastens the clasp to his helmet, and lifts it—but thinks better of it and leaves it on.

The air is cold and dank, just like the basement of his house. The old house has a constant problem with excess rainwater flooding the basement. Over the years, it painted wavy white lines along the base of the walls. His parents had installed a sump pump to help get rid of the water, but the problem had gone on for decades, and that unmistakable smell still lingered. It's like—UGH—the smell of the nosy old lady next door. A mixture of mildew and mold with a twist of pine cleaner—minus the pine cleaner. Put him anywhere with a blindfold on, and he'd be able to guess where he was. *Until now.*

A faint trickle of water drips like a spent faucet. *Drip. Drip. Drip.*

He's drawn to the far cave wall and studies thirteen neatly lined columns of tally marks. Each column has a few hundred tick marks. A sharp rock lies on the ground below. Chuckling, he picks it up and adds a few more to each column. He rubs the goosebumps on his bare arms, pulls them inside his shirt like a mummy, and treks further down the cave.

"Sully, I'm out of here if any vampire bats swoop down on me! My blood is just too precious!"

Massive stalactites and stalagmites stand at full attention on both sides of the cave. Their jagged appearance looks like the pointy teeth of a sand tiger shark. Peter shivers and imagines the cave walls opening and closing, gnawing, gnashing, and devouring anything that steps into their lair. If it came down to him or Sully, he'd feed the dog to the beast without a second thought! Quick to pass them, he follows the sound of the trickling water and stops in front of a brilliant blue subterranean river.

Peter notices gentle rippling circles casting out from the center of the river and waits, half expecting to see the water-loving dog emerge from its depths. With his eyes distracted from the cave floor for *just a moment,* his next step is onto a slimy, slippery patch of green moss that sends him theatrically flailing about. Had his arms not been tucked inside his shirt, they might have helped to balance him—or at least to break his fall.

CRASH! He hits the cave floor with a hard *THUD,* knocking the wind right out of him like a swift punch to the midsection. His screaming voice angrily reverberates off the cave walls. If someone did indeed have Sully, they now knew that Peter was there, too.

WHOOSH! At once, there's a flash, and an old man appears before him with a surprising start. Peter is still lying face down on the slippery cave floor. He lets out a soft moan and struggles to get his arms out of his shirt. He slowly gets up onto all fours, spits out some saliva layered with green moss, then stands and puts his hands on his lower back. Sully is standing directly behind the old man. His ears and muzzle droop down—his big eyes fix on the old man. The light from the torches cast dazzling rainbow colors off his collar. Had it always been this beautiful?

"Dude, how did you move so fast? You're so old. It was like the crack of lighting. Are you drinking the water down here or something? If so, can you bottle it for me?"

The old man lets out a chuckle and touches the helmet's spikes. He gently lifts Peter's chin with his ice-cold hand, and Peter lets out a dramatic shiver. The man's brilliant blue eyes stare deeply into Peter's big, dopey, brown ones.

Peter says, "Dude, your eyes are a bit maddening. It feels like I'm looking at one of those optical illusions that spin around in black and white circles: you try to look away. Still, you can't seem to no matter how hard you try." Peter casts his hands to the side and theatrically wobbles around in an elongated circle.

The man says nothing.

"Whatever. Maybe you're a mute. Well, come here, Sully. Come on, boy. I came through that freakshow of a mirror for you."

Sully looks up at Peter and then over to the old man. The dog lets out a whimper and lowers himself to the cave floor—like the time when he had scarfed down an entire serving plate of pot roast and vegetables. The dog had been too bloated to budge even an inch—instead staying in the same place for two whole days. It served him right. Peter had to eat a peanut butter and jelly sandwich that night.

With murder in his eyes, Peter juts out his bottom jaw and demands through gritted teeth, "What did YOU do to him?"

The old man's long teeth look like the piercing fangs of a serpent. He lets out a cackle and says, "True power—spikey human—is not having to explain yourself. The canine feels it, but I know you can, too." He arches his white eyebrows and splays both hands.

Peter tilts his head to the side. Looks. Pauses. Tilts his head to the other side. "Yeah, yeah. Okay. But who exactly are you? You look, well, not invisible, but not quite normal either. No offense, but your white skin looks like you haven't seen the sun in almost as long as me. And how did you make Sully do that? Did someone teach you that? Can you teach me? What else can...?"

"*ENOUGH* with the questions!" The old man's voice echoes off the cave walls causing Peter's bottom lip to quiver. "Why adults are so quick to teach tiny humans how to talk is simply *be-yond my understanding*!"

"Okay, but I'm warning you now. If you broke my dog, YOU'RE potty training a new one for me. Got it?"

"Oh? Is that a threat, spiky human?"

Forcing his chin up, "I guess it is. You should know, though, I always get what I want. But you can just answer my questions *now* and save us both a lot of time and aggravation. I *always* figure things out. Or I just keep going until people get fed up and just tell me what I want to know."

"Always?"

"Well, most of the time. There is this one aggravating old woman."

Raising the side of his lip in disgust, he says, "An old woman bested you?"

"Um, well, she doesn't like me, and I don't know why."

"Is that important to you? Do you want people to like you?"

"Hardly, but there's just something about that woman."

Even in the dim light of the cave, Peter can see the man's eyebrows furrow and the twinkling of his captivating blue eyes. "I'm not the least bit surprised to hear that. But why must you be so full of questions?"

He swallows hard before answering, "That's a great question! You see..."

"That, spiky human, is what you call a rhetorical question. I'm not the least bit curious about the answer." Pointing at Peter and pantomiming his demands into a perfectly shaped triangle. "Now, YOU are going to help ME pass through THAT mirror."

"*Oh, am I?* And what's in it for me?"

The old man says nothing.

Peter continues with his onslaught of questions. "How can I possibly do that anyway? We can't exactly take a bus or call an uber," he snorts like a pot-bellied pig as he lets out a laugh.

Enunciating his every word, the old man says, "There you go again with the questions. It's like someone scratching their fingernails down a chalkboard."

Letting out an awkward laugh, "Ugh, yeah...sorry, well...maybe, no...definitely not."

The old man rolls his neck in a wide circle causing it to crack like the snapping sound of a handful of wishbones.

"Something tells me it won't be the last time you ask me questions after I *explicitly* tell you not to."

"No, that's easy. I definitely won't stop. It's like you're a psychic old man or something. Hey," he says in the voice of the robotic fortune teller game at the circus, "if I give you a quar-ter will you tell me my fortune?"

"We've wasted enough time. I need to get back there," the old man says as he points to the shed on the other side of the mirror. "It's time for me to take back what's MINE. What was taken from me so many years ago."

Speaking a mile a minute now, "Are you trying to say that the hunk-of-junk shed is yours? Did you own it or something before us?"

The old man stares, saying nothing.

"Well, you couldn't have. According to my parents, the shed was built at the same time as the house. And the house has been in our family for generations. But ..."

The old man holds up a hand and cuts him off. "Yes, it's true your home has been in your family since it was first built in 1845 by your great grandparents, Alfred and

Ida Bailey."

"Ida? Ida know what kind of name that is!"

"May I continue?" but not pausing to wait for an answer. The house is an old Victorian home with many hidden features built into it. When they died, it was passed down to Oliver and Olive Bailey, your grandparents."

"Oliver and Olive? Seriously! That's funny! You just can't make this kind of stuff up."

"Your grandparents passed the home down to your *mother*. But I digress. The answer to your question about four questions ago is…the world—spiky human—is mine."

"Okay, okay. Cool. Calm your horses! But you keep calling me *spiky human*. Why? I get the spiky part, but the human part is just weird. It makes it sound like you aren't human—or—something."

"If I'm not human, pray tell, then what *am I?* It looks to me like I am just a weak old man that's trapped inside a spooky cave all alone and in *desperate* need of your help."

"Yeah, that's silly. Okay, but I need to know some more about you before I agree to help."

"So…you choose death then?"

"Death? No, not so fast, Quick Draw McGraw. Thanks, anyway. But that answers my question. I wanted nothing to do with helping some goody-two-shoes like Tom and Kate. If you were, I'd just assume to leave your carcass here to hang with the stalls!"

"The stalls?"

"Yeah, the stalactites and stalagmites, naturally."

"And what is this Quick Draw McGraw?"

"Ugh, seriously? Not a *what*, old man, but a *who*. He is a dumb red-hat wearing, gun-toting, spur-wearing horse from the Wild West. Whenever he needed to get his gun out, he usually shot the wrong person. That's *you*...and *I'm* the wrong person."

"Dumb?"

"Don't worry! He had a best friend named Baba Looey, who was always there to save the day. That, old man, would be ME!"

"Oh, really? Those dummies sound before your time."

"Yes, but you'll find I'm a wealth of information. Plus, there's an app for everything. I've watched every cartoon since before you were born." He chuckles. "Wait, you're old. I might need to revise that."

"And was this *Baba Looey* an animal, too?"

"Um, yeah."

"What kind?"

"He's a...a...a Mexican donkey. But it's more about how he helps Quick Draw McGraw, not that he's a donkey."

The old man's lips purse, and he slaps his hand over his mouth. His skinny stomach begins to bounce. After an awkward pause, he says, "I see. And exactly who are Tom and Kate? More animals?"

"Ugh, in a sense. Those are my parents."

"Interesting. And to get back on track, I have NEVER been called a goody-two-shoes before in my *entire* life."

"Well, you're old...so that's saying something. Okay then, I'll help you get through the mirror, but I have conditions. You might want to take some notes right beside all those tally marks you made on the wall. What are they for, anyway?"

The old man stares at Peter with his radiant blue eyes and slowly taps the tips of his ice-cold fingers together.

"Dude, you should be careful tapping your fingers like that. They're so cold they might snap off like icicles."

The old man stares right through him.

"Okay, keep your secrets then. And now for my list of demands..."

He lets out a violent laugh, and a large teardrop escapes down his wrinkled face. "A list?"

Peter holds up one finger and says, "Sully must come with us." Holding up a second finger, he says, "You must teach me how..."

Cutting Peter off mid-demand, the old man drawls, "You have a devil-may-care attitude indeed if you wish to insert yourself into *my world*. I only agree to allow the dog to come with us. The rest is yet to be determined *IF* and *WHEN* I teach you."

"Yes! So I'll take that as a maybe. Sweet! Okay, we—we it is!"

"Are you French?"

"Um...I dunno."

"What about your—*parents*?" asks the man. Elongating his next question, "Won't they be *worried* about you?"

"Pft! What about them? They don't care about me, and I *really* don't care about them," snaps Peter. "In fact, I HATE THEM! I want them to pay for not helping me. Can we add that to my list?"

"Indeed, we can. So, you agree to come with me *freely* then?" asks the old man as he pushes down his upwardly curving lips as they begin to form an ill-mannered smile.

"Yeah! Is that even really a question?"

"Yeah, *what*?" retorts the old man.

"Ugh—now you sound like my teacher. You're not going to do that all the time, are you?"

"I might. Or if you don't like that, you are free to stay

with your *parents,* whom you love *so* dearly!"

"Well, when you put it like that, you can correct me all you want. Yes!" lowering the pitch of his voice mockingly just like he does with his teacher, he says, "I agree to come with you," says Peter.

"*Freely?*" the old man says while motioning with his hands for him to finish.

"Yeah, yeah, yeah. You know, I should charge you for my awesomeness."

"You already have, child."

"What do you mean? How could I have charged you anything? We just met."

"Another time. Now, please finish what you were saying. In its entirety, if you don't mind."

Sully finally stirs and bolts out from behind the old man, slamming into Peter and knocking him to the ground. Peter turns to the dog and yells, "Oh, so now you want to play? Now that I'm not paying any attention to you. Figures!"

He pushes Sully to the side, causing the dog to slip on the wet cave floor and spin in a few rapid circles before slamming into a stalagmite. Peter rolls his eyes in disgust and says, "That serves you right for not coming to me when I first got here."

The old man reaches out and grabs both of Peter's hands. "Please proceed."

"I agree to come with you *freely,*" he says glibly to the old man.

After Peter utters those fateful words, the flames on the torches begin to flicker and nearly extinguish. Shadows dance along the cave walls. Peter struggles to break free of the old man as he instinctively tries to duck down.

"What are you doing?"

"Dude, the lights are flickering. I don't want a bat to get stuck in my beautiful hair!"

"Do you remember you're still wearing a spiky helmet?"

Letting out an awkward chuckle, he says, "Oh, yeah. That's right."

Sully lets out a sharp and agonizing cry from his tangled mess of legs as he lies helpless on the cave floor. He tries to stand several times but keeps falling back to the hard cave floor. He starts to get one leg up, then a second, and a third before slamming back to the floor—letting out a pained cry.

Peter does a whole-body shiver. It feels like ice is running through his veins—coursing and snaking throughout the rest of his body ending with the deep crevices of his dirty little toes. He can feel the pulsing of his wildly beating heart ringing loudly in his ears.

Baboom, baboom, baboom!

Each vertebra in his back feels like it's popping—like it's coming to life for the first time.

Pop, pop, pop!

It sounds like someone is progressively popping a stretch of bubble wrap. Like his body has a mind of its own, apart from Peter's consciousness. Once the old man lets go, Peter quickly extends his arms out and turns his palms face up. He rubs one against the other. Vigorously shakes them, then balls them up and roughly rubs his eyes. He shakes his hands again and then uses them to fan his burning eyes.

"Dude, my eyes are on FIRE! What's happening?"

Smiling, the old man replies, "You are becoming..."

"Becoming what? Enflamed? Did you set me on fire or something?"

"Silly, spiky child, you are not on fire. That's all I will say for now. Now, will you stop with the constant questions?"

"No, I won't ask you *no questions,*" promises Peter as he does the two-finger Cub Scout salute.

"You're not flashing some secret gang sign at me, are you?"

"You *really do* need me! First, you didn't know about Quick Draw McGraw and his trusty sidekick Baba Looey. Now you've never heard of the two-finger Cub Scout salute. Oh, the humanity," he says as he slaps his forehead with the pack of his hand. "You've clearly been in this cave for far too long."

"Okay," responds the man, "it might be helpful to have a tiny spiky human with me."

"Great! Hey, what's your name?"

Chapter 5

Peter gazes into the drab, old mirror. He does a quick wink at the reflection of the two of them staring back at him. The old man reaches out and grasps Peter's hand again. It still feels cold and creepy—yet this time, the two oddly fit together like a form-fitting glove. Peter nearly trips as he steps onto one of his untied shoelaces just as the two are about to pass through the mirror. He squats down and uses his free hand to tuck his dangling shoelace into the side of his muddy shoe. When he looks back up, his reflection is G-O-N-E! Only the old man's reflection remains.

"Hey, where's my...," but Sully manages to get up and is now on a full-out sprint. He knocks right into the back of Peter's legs, which would have sent him flying alone into the mirror but for the man's sturdy grasp of his hand.

Instead, they step together towards the mirror. Just like before—there's a brilliant bright flash of white light. WHOOSH! A weird sensation courses through Peter, almost like the feeling of rubbing a balloon on your hair to pick up static electricity and then sticking it to your shirt—times 100.

Presto—now they're on the other side of the mirror, standing back in the shed. Peter jumps as a spider glides down on and lands on his shoulder. Its piercing fangs are at the ready and about to pierce Peter's flesh when the old man makes a strange face. Then nothing. The spider is gone.

Peter turns back and looks at the mirror again, still seeing just one image. But now he can't see the cave from the shed. He shakes his head as he looks down at their grasped hands, still like a glove. But now the old man's hand feels warmer, not ice-cold like it had.

The old man's posture is different, too. He was closer to Peter's height just a moment ago when he was all hunched over like the Hunchback of Notre Dame. Now, the man towers over him like the pictures tracing prehistoric man's evolution to today's tall figures. The man's eyes are a penetrating ice blue. *His hair, wasn't it just grayed a minute ago?* Now it's long and blond with a golden sheen to it. Did Rumpelstiltskin have the man's hair spontaneously spun into gold or something?

In a sense, the man is strikingly beautiful. He looks like he should be on a magazine cover. Not the crazy tabloids in the grocery store checkout line of a man with three heads, all from different species, but a magazine cover boasting the world's most beautiful people.

Peter watches the man's reflection in the mirror as he drops his hand. And just like that, his own reflection returns. It's as if Peter just sidestepped right out of the man. Like he was inside, and now he's out—like a magical two-step dance. Or maybe even an alien emerging from the ripped open flesh of someone's stomach and pulling apart the rib cage for a light afternoon snack. Perhaps he should have flossed with the man's rib bone.

Speaking a mile a minute, Peter says, "Dude, that's so weird! I'm not a vampire or something now, am I? I didn't see my reflection a minute ago." Sizing the old man up and down, "Wow, it looks like passing through that ugly mirror did you a world of good! Can you teach Kate that anti-aging trick? She can use a tip or two! She's looking a bit *long in the tooth* lately. Get it? *Long in the tooth* because YOU just were—and now you're not. Did you suck those chompers in through your gums or something? Can you just spit them out like a Pez dispenser? And if I'm a vampire too, I should go now and feast on Kate and Tom! Or maybe the nosy neighbor. She's sure to be walking that foo-foo dog of her's."

The man lets out a chuckle. "Now that you're—*free*—so to speak, do you *still* want to go with me?"

"Ugh, well, where are you going?"

"I'm going to Amsterdam."

"Wow! Amsterdam, Netherlands! Sweet! I've never been out of the country! Hey, do I need a passport because I don't have one? That could be a problem. Can you get me one? But if I am a vampire, can't we just fly there? How long would that take? What do your wings look like? What...."

"No, child. You are not a vampire. We are going to Amsterdam, New York."

The man hangs his head down and shakes a bit as his shoulders fall up and down. "Before we leave, you must first do something. I need you to take all the money you can get from your," clearing his throat, "*from your parents.*"

"But what if they see me? They won't let me go with you! I'll be totally grounded for like— forever! Or at least until I look as old as you looked just a minute ago," he says with a chuckle at his own wit.

"Simple! You just can't let them see you."

"Ugh! You aren't the most helpful person. You know that already though, right? Fine! But keep Sully here with you."

Peter theatrically gets on his tiptoes and quietly leaves his bedroom, sticking his tongue out as he goes. His first stop is to his parents' bedroom. He picks up his father's work pants and removes the thick maroon wallet from his back pocket. He opens it up and carefully extracts the paper from the billfold.

"Let's see...20, 30, 35...$36. That's it! Geez, he's a walking advertisement to stay in school!" He shoves the money into his pocket.

The next stop is his mother's purse. She usually keeps it in the laundry room, which is right off the kitchen.

"Hmm, this isn't going to work."

He throws his giraffe-looking neck around the bend in the staircase. Stops. Turns back. Then heads towards the upstairs fire exit with the metal spiral staircase. He had guilted his parents into installing it for safety reasons a couple of years ago, but he had ulterior motives.

"As they say, this isn't my first rodeo."

He looks down and takes a deep breath. Then grips the staircase's cold metal bars and climbs down, placing one shaky foot after the other on the same step before continuing, looking like he did as an uncoordinated toddler first learning to walk up and down steps. Once down, he takes a big breath and wipes the sweat dripping from his forehead, not realizing he had been holding his breath. He gets on tiptoes and creeps around to the side of the house. The nosy neighbor is there again walking her prissy little dog, Miss Darcy. She peers in his direction, but he stays put and waits for her to pass.

"Geez, it's like that nosy old bat can smell me or something," he says to himself as he lifts his arms and sniffs his armpits for the second time that day.

Once she's gone, he continues around the outside of the house and stops at the rusty shed. He steps onto the door again and reaches for the plastic milk crate decorated nicely with an artful array of spiderwebs. He carries it outside, puts it just below the laundry room window, steps up, and lifts the old window. Grabbing the windowsill with both hands, he pulls his body up and goes through the window with the stealth of a prowler—until his sweaty hands lose their grip. He falls to the floor with a THUD. He stays there.

Motionless.

Listening.

Waiting.

Nothing.

He looks around and spots her purse exactly where he was expecting to see it. He pulls out her thin black wallet, removes $100 from the billfold, and puts it in his pocket. Plunging his hands deep into the purse, he pushes the contents aside until he finds her bright red liquid lipstick. He pulls the top and spills the liquid as though drizzling icing on a cake.

Next, he steals a glance past the laundry room door. His mother is sprawled out on the kitchen floor, resembling a child's yoga pose—her forehead pressed against the black and white tiled floor. Her hands are drawn out in front of her, painted with deep red and white splotches. She's muttering to herself. He inches closer until he can make out some of what she's saying.

"I failed. I promised. I'd put an end to this. I'm weak. It's happening. Again. I failed. I failed. I failed."

The local news blares from the living room television; the sound challenged only by his father's loud snoring. Peter can imagine his typical evening newspaper comically flying up and down with each passing snore. He would laugh if he didn't hate him so much right now.

Shaking his head, Peter mutters, "Now, will you look at that. That man couldn't care less that I'm gone."

Already lingering too long, he rushes to the window but notices the nosy neighbor on her way back this time. He quietly steps behind the solid gray curtains and waits for her to leave. Then he gently lifts the bottom of the window and climbs back out—returning the crate to the shed.

Twenty minutes later, he finds himself scampering back up the spiral staircase and through the second-story door. Returning to his bedroom, he whispers like a troll, "Here's—all—I—could—get! Um—*old-young* man—*young-old* man—where'd you go?"

He looks around and spies the man sifting through his parents' filing cabinet in the study across the hall. It's the one room in the house his father was able to design himself. Proud wooden bookshelves line every wall. Each book reverently touched time and time again. Respected. Nestled in its own special place.

There's an impressive collection of first edition books.

His father had this corny habit of putting on a dress jacket before he even touched them. He explained to Peter that he always felt like he was right beside the authors because they were the first books printed of that particular title.

He has classics ranging from William Shakespeare to Charles Dickens to Edgar Allan Poe. He once watched his father shed a tear as he reached the end of John Steinbeck's novel *Of Mice and Men.* Peter had angrily snatched the book out of his father's hands and quickly flipped to the end of the story to see what had made him so upset.

"So!" scoffed Peter, "the dumb oaf was killed by his friend. End of story. Move on already!"

His father had responded, "I don't expect you to understand the depths of friendship and mercy. You are capable of neither. I knew that when we first got you."

"Got me? Don't you mean *had me?* That's how it works you know."

"Yeah...um...right. *Had you.*"

Now, Peter says to the man, "Dude, I can promise you there's NOTH-ING interesting in *there*! That's where interesting things go to," spelling it out, "D-I-E!"

"Well, do you have it?"

"Yes, yes. It's not much, though. You see, I pride myself on spending their money as fast as I can."

"Okay, well, *that's* a fun fact. By the way, my name is Bael. Let's go!"

Chapter 6

Bael, Peter, and Sully leave the Powell House with their pilfered money. The late summer sun casts a long, thin shadow announcing the nosy neighbor, followed by her prissy little dog, Miss Darcy.

"Hide!" Peter begs.

Bael replies dryly, "I hide from no mortal, especially when they're walking an ankle-biter donning a pink tutu."

Shrugging his shoulders, he says, "Okay, I can see your point."

The nosy neighbor stops right in front of them, wrinkles her nose, and asks with disdain, "Where is THAT dog's leash? If I've told you once, I've told you a hundred times!"

Peter feigns fear for a split second then asks, "And I want to know where THAT dog's self-respect is. I mean really—a pink tutu. You *both* have issues!"

Looking indignant, she huffs, "Well, I never!"

"Of course," Peter stands taller and moves in front of Bael, "*you never* because you're always busy pretending to walk your stupid little dog so you can spy on me. You don't have time to do anything else."

"Well, *somebody* has to protect people from the likes of YOU!"

"But I'm just a kid."

"JUST a kid? I think not. Especially now that the past has come back to haunt us. It's inevitable, I'm afraid." Turning towards Bael, she cups her hands in front of her eyes and says, "And I thought *you* were gone for good!"

Bael turns to the woman and says in a low drawl, "You have said quite enough already, Yarin. It's time for you to be on your way."

She pulls her large purse close to her chest and storms off in her white orthopedic Velcro shoes, looking over her shoulder and casting dirty looks at him every few steps until she is just outside the Powell House.

Peter asks Bael, "I wonder if she's going to stop at my house and tell my parents."

"Do you care if she does?"

"No, not really. But I wanted to make them wonder what happened to me. Maybe they'd think I was kidnapped or something. You know—really make them sweat. Yarin. Was that her name?"

"Yes."

Chuckling, "I always called her the nosy neighbor. Funny, I knew her dog's name, though."

Bael smiles, and they walk to the end of the cul-de-sac. Once the sidewalk ends, they trek onto a well-traveled dirt path used by the neighborhood kids looking for a shortcut on their travels to and from school. It was also a place away from the watchful eyes of the nosy neighbor. The neighborhood kids were quite disappointed when just last week, Miss Darcy had pulled away from the woman and darted onto the path, revealing their secret lair.

The path is thick with lush vegetation and ripe with bloodthirsty mosquitoes getting ready for their nightly feeding frenzy. Sully spins in circles one way and alternates directions as he tries to keep the gnats from landing on his rear-end. Peter laughs as several gnats land on the dog's butt, causing him to quickly sit down and drag his rump across the ground, trying to get them off. Suddenly the gnats change their trajectory. Peter lets out an ear-piercing scream as they charge towards him like a bull, landing right in his open mouth and eyes.

"Ugh!" he screams—and gags as he unwittingly lets in another gnat—closes his mouth fast—swallows it by sheer reflex—and smacks a mosquito buzzing around his face leaving a trail of crimson on his cheek. We've been walking on this path for *hours*! I'm not going to have any blood left." Out of breath, "Are—we—almost—there—yet?"

Speaking dryly, "No, definitely not. We most certainly are *not* almost there yet."

"What!" Peter continues to smack himself silly. "I thought this is the part where adults are supposed to lie to you and tell you—*yes, honey—we're almost there*!"

Bael manages a smirk, "Would you like me to lie to you?"

Tilting his head to the side like Sully does, Peter says, "Uh, I don't know. Let me think about that. Hey, *why* aren't these tiny vampires sucking your blood OR flying into your eyes and mouth?" Letting out a snort, he says, "Or does my blood just taste better?"

"Those *tiny vampires* know better than to try and bite me."

"What do you mean by that?"

Bael tilts his head to the side and says nothing. He stares deeply at a mosquito on the tip of Peter's nose.

"Now, don't move."

Peter goes cross-eyed as he tries to look at the bloodsucker perched on his nose like a skydiver going down for the plunge. Its brown body changes to a brilliant, sparkling gold. Did he make a mistake? Was he looking at a firefly and *not* a bloodsucker? Suddenly, its entire body engulfs in fire, and it lifelessly falls into Peter's open hand, much like the drifting embers of a campfire.

"Hey!" he screams as he violently shakes the smoldering remains from his hand. "What did you do that for?"

"It's just a glimpse of what I can do—for now..."

"Dude, haven't you already figured out that you can't just give me a glimpse of anything! I'm proud to say I have the patience of a 2-year-old."

"That thought did cross my mind."

"Will you teach me how to do that?"

"I will, but you must first gain your strength."

"No problem. Should we stop and get some cans of spinach?"

"Why would we do that?"

"You know, like Popeye."

"Is that another donkey?"

"Ha ha! No, he's a sailor that eats spinach, and his muscles blow up like the Incredible Hulk."

"So, is THAT a donkey?"

"No! He's a green superhero. Well, he's really Dr. Bruce Jenner, but turns into the green monster when he gets upset."

Rolling his eyes and clicking his tongue on the top of his mouth, Bael replies, "Intriguing."

Meanwhile, Sully's mouth keeps opening and snapping shut as he tries to catch the mosquitos buzzing around his head.

Peter asks, "Hey, have you ever read the story *Why Mosquitos Buzz in People's Ears*?"

"I can't say I've had the pleasure."

"Well...it's because THEY'RE SUPER ANNOYING. I'm TIRED. And if we don't stop soon, you're going to find out why I buzz in YOUR EARS!"

"Okay! Okay! Okay! I can't take your whining anymore! You win! We'll stop somewhere for the night."

"Man! It took you long enough to catch on! I *tried* to tell you when we first met."

"You couldn't talk when we first met. You were..."

Cutting him off, Peter says, "I know. Cut me some slack, Jack. I had just fallen on the wet cave floor. *You* should have been a better host and put down one of those gripper things you find in showers to prevent just such a thing. You probably want to start taking notes. I have a lot of wisdom to share with you."

Bael shakes his head at Peter's comment but quickly smiles when he hears the buzz of the neon hotel sign brilliantly flashing *"VACINSIE."* They approach the hotel lobby without another person in sight other than the oblivious desk clerk who is captivated with a reality television show featuring a man wearing a penguin suit with a rose in his mouth and desperately looking for a wife.

The hotel's best days are behind it. It had thrived in the small river town with a booming industrial climate seeking a cheap water source for transportation and the spilling of its factory waste downriver. But the factories have long since left for more affordable production elsewhere. Now, vacant buildings occupy more space than even people do. Signage lines the river indicating that the water is not safe to swim in, and the fish are not safe to eat.

Peter chuckles, "I bet you this lady has been drinking the water!" Not waiting for a response, Peter's eyes widen as he looks at the TV, "With any luck, that guy will get pricked by one of those thorns from the rose he's holding in his mouth. Maybe we'll see some blood from someone else other than *me* tonight."

Bael turns to Peter and says, "I'll do all of the talking. Understand?"

Throwing his arms to his side, he puffs, "The *indignity*! You act like I like to interrupt people or something."

"Or *something* indeed."

Bael approaches the snaggle-toothed desk clerk who is animatedly screaming at the penguin on TV to choose the woman in the red dress. He clears his throat to get her attention. She holds up her index finger with her gaze not leaving the television screen. He clears his throat even louder the second time. Her face contorts, and she half-heartedly forces herself to look away from the television.

"Yeah, yeah. The restroom is that way," and she points to the toilet sign. The overbite of her top teeth gripping her bottom lip causing the pink to fade to white.

She misses what the penguin just said and feverishly combs her hands through her hair. She tries to look back at the television, but Bael is now holding her gaze with his striking blue eyes, so she resorts to biting her nails instead. She tears a sliver off and spits it onto the counter.

Peter exclaims, "Gross! Are you trying to spell a word with your chewed up and spit out pieces or something? If that's the case, you should stick to sunflower seeds then."

Bael says, "That's a filthy habit. But for what it's worth, I seem to have your attention *now*." He says condescendingly, "I'd like a room for the night."

"Yes, sirree, Joe Bob." says the clerk. "One room for you and your son comin' up!"

"What are you talking about? His name isn't Joe Bob!" yells Peter. "And he's not..."

Bael turns to Peter and fights back a laugh. Sully moans, almost like even the dog knows that Peter should shut up. Peter seems to understand this now, too, and promptly gets to the business of shutting up.

Turning to Peter, "Hey there, little mister. I didn't mean to offend you none." Returning to Bael, "That will be 80 buck-a-roos. Sorry, we don't take any of those credit card thingies. Good old American cash-ola only," proudly proclaims the clerk.

Bael looks deeply into her heavily lined brown eyes. Judging by her appearance, her bloodline includes raccoons possibly crossed with clownfish. His eyes pulsate again and he commands her, "No, you will not charge us for the room. You will even give us the BEST room you have AND a free dinner delivered to us. Throw in a water bowl and a bone for the dog, too. Do you understand?"

Peter screams, "Sully shouldn't drink the water. Add bottled water. We don't want him looking like *this lady* here now, do we? His teeth already kind of do!"

The hotel clerk's face reddens, and her shoulders

slump. Her head begins to bob up and down like an absent-minded buoy in the middle of a lake. Though speaking to Bael, her gaze goes right past him.

"Do you want French fries or onion rings with your dinner?"

"Both! Both! He wants both!" screams Peter. "He also wants an ice cream sundae with extra hot fudge!"

She drawls, "Yes."

Her skin is clammy as she hands Bael the keys to room 113, not blinking even once. Their room faces the pool encircled by a lazy river with a gigantic three-story waterslide right in its belly. Peter perks up but then quickly drops his head. The waterslide has an "out of order" sign. The pool water is lime green and looks like snot. And the lazy river is hospitable to a menagerie of loudly croaking frogs. So, unless your Shrek, you wouldn't like it. Bummer!

"Hey, that lady was in a trance. Not saying that she's working with much of a brain, but how did you do that?" asks Peter.

He waits, but Bael doesn't respond.

"Why did you ask me to take my parents' money then? You didn't need it. They could have caught me! You could have been seen. Sully could have barked."

Bael's body goes rigid. "I thought you weren't going to ask me any more questions."

"Well, what I *actually* said was that I wouldn't ask *no questions*. See, it's a double negative. To not ask no questions means to ask questions," Peter says as he puffs up his chest and flashes a broad smile.

"Fine. It's because I don't like your," he swallows hard, *"parents."*

"Neither do I, but what's your reason?"

"Well, most people value money above all else. I didn't need it, but they did. That's why I had you take it."

"Oh. I get it, but why don't *you* like them?"

"They took things from me."

"I get it! Now you want to take something from them. Well, you should have told me. My mother likes this stupid necklace that belonged to my grandmother. She protects it like it's magical or something. I would have taken that, too. It's probably worth a pretty penny."

Bael's face lights up at the mention of the necklace. "Do explain."

"See, it means that something costs a lot."

"NO! Explain what the necklace looks like."

Chuckling and letting out a snort, "Oh, yeah, okay. Well, it's kind of silver. Or maybe gold. It has a large stone thingy on the front. I tried to touch it once, but Kate took it away and ordered me never to touch it again. Of course, I looked for it again, but she hid it so hard that I couldn't find it, and that's saying something."

"What happened when you touched it?"

"Keep up, Jack! I just told you, she yelled at me."

"No, that's not what I meant. What did it *feel* like?"

"Like a necklace."

Smacking his forehead with a smart whap, "Did it feel powerful at all? Did you feel powerful touching it?"

"Oh, well, why didn't you say so? I was surprised when Kate yelled at me, but I remember the room seemed warmer. Sully woke up and came running into the room at just around the same time. I remember it clearly because he followed me out of the room when Kate kicked me out. The stupid dog tripped me and then pounced right on top of me. It hurt! Then he did this maniacal sniffing thing. I lost my favorite penny slug because he tore a hole right in my pocket. I had hundreds of free games at the Barrel of Fun Arcade with that thing. I was so mad!"

With Bael's eyes fixed on him, he continues blabbering. Why waste a captive audience, after all.

"Hey, what makes a penny pretty anyway? They seem pretty dirty and have this weird coppery smell."

Bael just shakes his head. They enter the hotel room. "It's cold in here!" whines Peter.

"Adjust the air conditioner."

"I have a better idea. Look at that fireplace. We should roast some marshmallows. Have you ever had smores?" Peter asks excitedly. Looking around, "Bummer! I don't see any way to start a fire."

"That's because it's summer, and they don't want you using it. It would be a waste of money to air-condition the room."

"Are you afraid to break the rules or something? Remember what I said about goody-two-shoes? Do I need to renegotiate our agreement?"

"As if you could! Okay, take Sully outside and find some wood."

"I'm on it."

"Come on, Sully!" calls Peter.

He grabs a stick off the ground and taunts the dog with a game of fetch. He pulls his arm back and pretends to throw it into the tall brush. Sully excitedly cries out and runs after it. The songbirds suddenly stop singing as the dog animatedly jumps around, barks wildly, and crunches the leaves on the ground during his search. He finds one and returns to Peter. He pulls hard, removes the stick from the dog's mouth, and does the same thing again. Sully again runs into the brush looking for the stick. The two repeat this until Peter has a collection of a dozen sticks.

He lets Sully keep his thirteenth finding, which is less of a stick and more of a long branch. Peter opens the hotel door. Sully is right behind him but can't make it through the door frame with the long branch. Every time he tries to step over the threshold, the branch hits the doorframe, and the dog bounces back. Too stubborn to drop the branch, he repeats his attempt with tiny splinters falling to the floor. He even tries to enter the room walking backwards, which gets more of his body into the room but still hits when the branch reaches the door frame. He angles the branch, shimmies and contorts his brindle body, and finally enters the room with the branch leading the way first, followed by him.

Peter haphazardly tosses the sticks he was holding into the fireplace without any apparent rhyme or reason. It looks like someone just opened a canister of *Pick Up Sticks* and threw them in.

"We need more wood. I want this to be BIG!"

Peter looks over at Sully's branch and reaches down to snatch it. Sully growls at him and covers it protectively with his two front paws.

"It will be fine, Peter."

Bael fixes his blue gaze upon the sticks in the fireplace. His body is motionless as his eyes start to pulsate different shades of brilliant blue. Smoke escapes from the dried-up wood and pours out like a faucet. Then—WHOOSH—a fire fills the full length of the fireplace like someone turned on a gas stove. Sully starts panting loudly as the heat quickly envelopes him.

"Cool! I'm with the ultimate fire starter! Hey, can I rent you out for parties and bar mitzvahs?"

Bael crosses his arms and says nothing. "Okay, okay. I was just joking! Don't get so bent out of shape about it."

"So you're not afraid that I can do that? What if I lit YOU on fire?"

"Dude, why would I be afraid? I'm going to make you teach me how to do that!"

Bael looks deeply into Peter's eyes and holds his gaze until Peter says, "No offense, dude, but that's *kind of creepy.*"

"Interesting. Tell me more about what you feel when I look directly into your eyes."

"Ugh, nothing. It just feels like I'm going past a bad car accident and can't help but look."

"Charming, but seriously, I think you just might have *it.*"

"Uh, have what? You can even check my pockets," Peter says as he turns them out.

"You're a weird child," Bael says as he tousles Peter's already messy hair. "Okay, first, you have to stare deeply at the object you wish to burn. Almost like you're looking directly through it."

"Like that clerk looked at you?"

"Yes. Then, take a deep breath and fill your body with air. Push it from your chest to your toes. Feel the burn within you. Next, use your inner core to force the fire out of you and onto whatever you wish to burn. Let it take control of the object and pour all your anger and rage into it, just like I did with the mosquito and now the fireplace."

"So, how do I make my eyes change the way yours do?"

"It will just happen."

"Okay. Just let me check my eyes out in the mirror first so I can see if they change just like yours do."

"NO!" screams Bael as he grabs Peter's arm before he can reach the mirror. Clearing his throat and getting control of himself, "Mirrors are a sort of *bad luck*. I'd prefer that we didn't use them."

"Okay, okay. No mirrors," Peter moans, "Woo! Woo!" as he holds up his hands and wiggles his fingers like he's a scary ghost. "Perfect, it just means I don't have to bother brushing my hair from now on."

Replying dryly, "Simply delightful, Peter. Simply delightful."

"But I *really* do want to know how you change your eyes. They flash these bright shades of blue like some kind of pulsating magnetic field moving in and out; only I know that they're not magnetic. Do you know what I mean?"

"That's not something I can teach you. It will come as you gain control over your thoughts and learn how to harness your powers. Now I must take care of something. Don't get into trouble while I'm gone."

"Say, what? I have powers?"

Bael opens the door and steps out of the hotel room for a few minutes. As the door opens, Peter can hear the croaking sound of the bullfrogs getting louder and louder. The melody is oddly inviting, and Peter tries to hop from bed to bed in sync with their *ribbit-ing* tune.

Meanwhile, Sully is whining in the corner and maniacally licking his front left paw until it's red and raw like a T-bone steak. Once the fun of jumping from bed to bed passes, Peter spends several minutes looking around for the remote control to the television. He lifts one of the tattered old comforters and looks under the bed. The mattress is sitting on top of a wooden plank that's nailed to the floor.

"Seriously! Who would want to steal this hunk of junk? Well, I guess maybe me because I would have used the *too-good-even-for-termites* wood for the fireplace."

He looks behind the dresser. BINGO!

The remote control is lodged between the two inches of space between the wall and the dresser. Peter tries to reach his arm behind the dresser, but it's not long enough. He paces around the room, smiles, but then quickly frowns. The clothes hangers are attached to the closet rod and can't be removed, lest any guest attempt to swipe one. Or burn one. He carefully checks them one at a time. He gets to the last one and discovers that it's loose. He yanks on it with all his strength, but nothing happens.

"This is a simple problem. I simply need the right motivation."

He pushes the hangers all the way to the side and begins singing, "George, George, George of the Jungle, watch out for that tree! Weee," he screams as charges at the hangers and swings on one like a vine.

With a crash and a thud, both Peter and the hanger fall to the ground. "Victory!" He climbs on top of the dresser and fishes the hanger down the wall. He hits the remote control like a golf ball. *"Fore!"*

He picks up the dusty remote control and attempts to turn on the television, but it doesn't work. He smacks it smartly and tries again. DOUBLE BINGO! The television turns on, and he catches a preview of the upcoming story about him and Sully on the Channel Nine Nightly News at 6:00.

"Breaking story. A 13- year-old boy, Peter Powell, is

missing along with his dog, Sully. The pair were last seen two days ago and believed to be runaways. Anyone with information about the missing boy and his dog are asked to call the local police department at the number listed on the bottom of your screen."

He throws the remote control against the wall sending the batteries and battery cover flying in opposite directions. Sully jumps at the loud sound.

"Now, will you see that! They didn't even offer a reward for us. Sully, don't cry to go back home—we don't have one! Like Bael said, people value money. They didn't offer any for us. They really don't care. There's the proof! And if I had any pudding, I'd give it to you right now."

Sully tilts his head to the side, trying to discern what Peter said.

"Keep up, dog. The proof is in the pudding! Get it?"

Peter stops watching the television and scans the room. Aside from the two beds, there are two nightstands, a small kitchenette, and a bathroom. He opens both nightstands and rummages through each. There are some takeout menus and a bible. He opens the minifridge and spies something that looks like beef jerky, long and wilted but smells like rotting fish. He flings it over the back of his shoulder and continues checking the drawers. Sully sees him toss the mystery meat and expertly catches it and scarfs it down in one fluid bite. Peter shakes his head,

"Oh well, I guess we'll have to wait on Bael for dinner." As the dog licks the crevices of his mouth, Peter screams, "UGH, Sully...tell me you didn't just eat that thing!"

Peter passes by an oversize, built-in mirror near the bathroom and does a double-take. "WHOA!" He rubs his eyes, closes them, then opens them again. His eyes—they aren't brown anymore—but they're not blue either. They are brown-ish with blue streaks shooting out from his dark black pupils to his cornea. Just then, the door clicks open, and he hurries away from the mirror.

"Hey," Peter says, "my eyes are..."

Bael asks, "Yes?"

"Oh, well...uh...they're tired. Are yours?"

"I see..."

Letting out a forced laugh, "I get it...you *see!*"

"Was there something *else* you wanted to tell me?

"Nope...just that my eyes are tired."

"Delightful."

Chapter 7

They barely touch their toes to the floor that morning when Peter cries out, "I'm starving! I'm wilting away to nothing. But don't worry, Bael," pinching the side of his stomach, "you have some reserves!"

Bael comically rolls his eyes and excuses himself. He returns a few minutes later carrying an armful of delectable food choices. "Do you know why this is quickly becoming my favorite time of the day?"

Peter belches loudly and talks with a mouthful of a bacon, egg, and cheese sandwich, "Huh?" and he accidentally inhales a bit of his sandwich and begins coughing.

"Attractive. It's one of the few times when you're not talking. Well, it was until now anyway."

Bael flings a sausage patty like a frisbee to Sully. RUFF! He swiftly catches the airborne pig disk and happily scours it down. He shakes his head in slow motion, and some multi-colored drool breaks off and smacks against the wall, and runs down with the thick, slow viscosity of snail goo—pulling some dust with it like a snowball picking up patches of dirt as it rolls downhill.

"Now, will you look at that. Sully has better table manners than you do."

Still talking with a mouthful, he says, "Good one! Hey," chomp, chomp, "why aren't you eating?"

"I don't eat."

"And you think *I'm* dramatic. You mean you don't eat what's here."

"No, I don't eat at all."

"Whoa! How do you live without food?"

"I...shall I say...get my energy a different way."

"What do you mean? A *different* way?" Peter asks as he emphasizes the word *different* and throws his hands up and pretends to be walking a catwalk like a fashion model.

"I feed off of...humans."

"Dude, please tell me you're not a zombie who wants to suck my brains out through my nasal passages!"

"No, I would starve..."

"Ha ha!"

"Okay, I feed off dark emotions. The stronger they are, the stronger I become."

"So, what about when you were in the cave? Weren't you alone? Why didn't you die?"

"It's true that I was there for an exceptionally long time. My strength had indeed diminished. It was you, Peter, who sensed me on the other side of the mirror, even if you didn't realize it at the time."

"I didn't even know you yet. How could I have possibly helped you?"

"You always knew that there wasn't a bond between

you and your," clearing his throat,

"*parents*. I could feel it through the mirror. For the longest time, I was curled up in a fetal position like a baby with my arms and legs pulled tightly to my chest. Unable to move. Once you turned thirteen, Peter, it was *you* who gave me strength. *You* who helped me to stand again. *You* who came through the mirror and brought me back, Peter."

"I did all that? So what happened before I turned thirteen? Did you just lie there and suck your thumb or something?"

"Charming, Peter. Simply charming. Anyway, now it's my turn to return the favor."

"Well, it's about time! You can start by getting us a car. And can we stop at someplace cool for lunch? I won't feel guilty picking the place on account of your," he sternly lowers his voice and says, "your *different energy source* and all. But seriously, can you get us a car? Ugh—I'd even settle for a bike. Make it a bicycle built for two. You can pedal when we go up hills. I will pedal when we go down them. Seems fair to me."

"I do understand your human legs are tired. It will pass. For now, Peter, I'm going to try something, but I need you to be absolutely still and quiet."

Gently taking Peter's hands into his, the boy breaks out into a fit of laughter.

"That tickles!"

"Peter!"

"Okay, okay. *Be still my beating heart.* Got it!"

"Alright, now..."

"WAIT!"

"What, Peter?"

"Do you even have a heart? I don't mean—swoon—like a teenage girl, do *you love me* kind of heart. I mean, do you have blood, a heart, and lungs? That kind of stuff?"

"Peter, if you don't stay still, I'm going to show you exactly what I have!"

Bael's eyes start to pulsate. Peter's body goes limp. His elbows and knees let out a soft crack and lock. Peter's eyes bulge to the size of saucers as Bael shrinks to his level. They're now nose-to-nose. No, wait. Bael didn't shrink. It's Peter who is the size of Bael. Not the other way around. Peter breaks their eye contact as he looks at his shoulders that now feel like inflatable swimmies. He was flying—no levitating. And his ears! They feel five times too big. Did he turn into Dumbo?

Gritting through his teeth, "HOLD—STILL—PETER!"

Bael resumes focusing on Peter's multicolored eyes. They begin to sting and fill up with uncontrollable tears that quickly run down his face. Embarrassed, he looks away. Bael lightly places his hand under Peter's chin and guides his face back up, so they are again staring eye to eye. Peter's eyes suddenly flash and pull in all the light around them, causing his brownish-blue eyes to transform into beautiful blue eyes, just like a butterfly emerging from a chrysalis.

SWOOSH! They were standing inside the hotel room in front of the heavy metal door—then suddenly appear outside by the loudly croaking frogs near the mildew-laden lazy river.

"WHOA! How did we do that? You mean we could have done that this whole time and you made us walk? I don't know if I should hug you or kick you!"

Bael chuckles, "No, Peter. We couldn't have done that

all along. You had to build up your strength. There are many things that I can teach you. This is just the beginning."

"Um, okay. But what about Sully? Can he do that thing with us?"

"Animals do not fall under the same rules as we do."

"Are we...um...magical?"

"Yes, Peter. We have special abilities that humans do not."

"I WAS RIGHT! YOU AREN'T HUMAN!"

"I repeat what I said in the cave. If I'm not human, then what am I?"

"Well, okay, let's see then. You were old, and now you're young. No, make it younger, you're still an old dude. Your hair is long and blond. I played with a fallen strand of it when you weren't looking."

"Are you serious?"

"Yes, I was bored. SHHH! Now, before I was so rudely interrupted, I was saying your hair is long and blond. It's extraordinarily strong. I used a few strands of it to make a sort of guitar. Sully didn't enjoy listening to my musical melodies and kept howling, so I stopped. You have these long, pointy ears. You can control minds, but not mine. It must be because of my exceedingly high level of intelligence! And I'm not sure what we just did, but we were in the hotel room, and now we're outside."

"I repeat, what am I?"

"I'm still working that out."

"Let me help you. I'm an elf."

"I told you back in that cave that I wouldn't help you if you were a goody-two-shoes! You lied! Now I find out you're some magical fairy or something."

"I'm an elf. A *dark* elf."

"Whoa! That's more like it."

Bael smacks his lips. "I'm glad I meet with your approval."

"Wait. Does that mean that I'm a dark elf, too?"

"Yes."

"What about Tom and Kate?"

With a sharp flash of his eyes, he grits his teeth and seethes, "They share NOTHING in common with me!"

"Thank the dark elf god for that!"

"Indeed."

"So can you..."

"That's enough for now."

"But how..."

"Peter!"

Talking exceptionally fast to get the question out, "Hey, how did Sully get outside with us?"

"Fine. Sully is an exceptional animal. I knew that the minute he came through the mirror. As long as he is standing within an arm's length of me, he can follow us anywhere we go. So, back to what I was trying to show you in the first place. Would you like to walk in the human realm or the faster way?"

"Hello, McFly! Why are you even asking me such a ridiculous question? You know how lazy I am! Duh...the faster way."

"Let's go, then." Bael grasps Peter's hands.

Suddenly it feels like they are riding a zero-gravity ride at an amusement park. Peter's face feels like it's elongating and stretching like it's on a pottery wheel. His eyes feel like they are spinning in 360 degrees like two basketballs on the tip of a finger. He's afraid to blink out of fear they will permanently roll right into the back of his head. Just when he feels like he can't take it anymore, they stop outside what the sign calls *"The Amsterdam Foster Care Regional Office."* Just as Bael had explained, Sully appears right beside them.

Peter cries out, "I think I'm going to be..." and he vomits all over Bael's neatly polished shoe. But it just runs right off the shoe like water running down a window. He gets overly excited at seeing the vomit just slide right off of Bael's shoe and vomits all over again. Learning from the first episode, Bael quickly moves his foot out of Peter's line of fire.

Once the vomiting subsides, Peter joins Bael on a bench just outside the building. Peter drops his elbows to rest on his knees—his face cradled in his hands. The color slowly returning to his pallid face.

"So, what are we doing NOW? Please tell me that we aren't just going to sit here! UGH! You'd better be careful, or you'll turn old again! Even worse, what if *I* turn old, too! Oh, the humanity!"

Bael's face contorts. Gritting his teeth, he responds, "The humanity INDEED. I am thinking of the best way that I can help some *unfortunate* children."

"Dude, I've got mad skills! *You* even said so. We make a great team."

"Team?"

"Uh huh! Someone's gotta be the brains behind this operation! If you think about it, I already started when I helped you from the other side of the mirror. I'm happy to accept the job. By the way, how much does it pay?"

Chuckling, he says, "We are going inside at the shift change in the morning."

"What exactly is it that we're doing? And why on earth are we waiting until morning?"

"You are going to pretend to be my adopted son. I own a farm, and we need some extra farmhands to help run it. The children will go to school. You go to school, too. Do you understand?"

"Hey! You own a farm? Can we go there?"

"Stick to the story."

"Am I a good student? Because my teachers always love me. I'm good at making people believe what I want them to believe. Hmm—I guess I have some mind control powers of my own."

"Indeed..."

"Do I call you Dad?"

"Peter!"

"Yeah, yeah! Farm! School—maybe a good student! You're my new dad! I don't know what I call you yet! Maybe dad, maybe not! Old man, young man! Got it!"

Bael puts his head down, covers his face, and his body starts to bounce slightly.

"Hey! Are you actually *laughing?* Totally creepy, dude! Stick to the scare tactics! And why do we have to wait? The door says they're open 24-hours a day. Makes sense if they're dealing with kids who are in trouble with the law."

"Stick to the plan."

"Whatever!"

Peter picks his legs up and gets comfortable on the bench. The sun goes down, and the temperature cools. Bael notices him shivering and drapes an arm around his shoulders. Peter turns his face into Bael's shoulder and falls fast asleep. He wakes to a puddle of drool on Bael's shoulder and an annoying bird chirping in his ears.

Peter whines, "I'm hun..."

Bael tosses a granola bar at Peter, who snatches it right up. Bael walks up a few concrete steps leading to a set of glass double doors and reaches his arm out but quickly extracts it like he just touched something hot.

Baring his teeth, he seethes, "Sully, stop that!"

Peter looks at the dog and starts laughing so hard he doubles over and grabs his stomach in a wild fit of hysteria. He then chokes on the granola bar and begins a fantastic coughing fit. Sully was standing there with one leg in the air and was just about to *mark* the weeds growing up through the cracks in the cement.

"Errow," which must be dog speak for, "What did I do?"

He put his leg down just in time before being noticed by a woman inside who was in the middle of pointing her finger into the faces of four oversize men. The men were fervently bobbing their heads up and down with dropped, sunken shoulders—their hands neatly folded in front of them. The woman mouths something, and the four men turn their gaze to the door. She throws her upturned hands into the air—points her nose upward—and heads towards the handsome man standing at the door.

The woman dons a long silk trench coat with a matching floral print silk chiffon beret. She squares her body up, causing her chest to comically puff up, accentuating her obtuse stomach that hangs out further than her legs are long. Her beady eyes squint as she prepares for battle. Peter at once recognizes this.

"Sssp, Bael, Dad, or whatever. She looks like she wants to leave. You might want to show her that you can do something for her. Just saying."

"Stick—to—the—plan!" Bael says through gritted teeth.

In a shrill voice, she says, "Look, whoever you are, we don't have any money. In fact, if we owe you money, you're not going to get it, so you're just—just wasting your time. You'll need to get in line," bellows the Portly Lady. "I'm entitled to MY paycheck!"

Bael pulls out a monetary donation by way of Peter's parents. "Hello. My name is Bael. Ma'am, I don't have much, but something told me I simply must stop on my journey and offer it to you. Please accept this small token of what I can offer you towards your well-deserved salary."

"You mean we don't owe *you* money?" she asks incredulously as her war pose relaxes, and she leans in closer to this strange man.

"No, ma'am. I just want to help. Kids are expensive, and good help doesn't come cheap."

"You're telling me!" as she turns to the staff and rolls her eyes at them. "We've had to get, well, rather creative just to stay afloat. These good-for-nothing kids would be begging for change on a street corner if it wasn't for me!"

"Your kindness, Mr. Bael, is very, very much appreciated. Is there something I can do for you?" asks the Portly Lady. "The children are particularly good at making sandwiches. I'm sure they can also find something tasty for your dog, too."

"No thank you, kind ma'am."

"But...but..."

Stomping on Peter's foot, "Like I was saying, I'm a simple man. I own a farm and need some extra farmhands to help me run it. You see, I adopted this boy right here and his dog."

"Adopted? That's so kind of you! Why he looks just like you, though! Do you have any children of your own?"

His eyes narrow, and his back stiffens. She quickly adds, "Not that it makes you any less of a parent. I—I just wondered if there were more children in your home in addition to this boy."

"I understand why you ask. Yes. Yes, I do."

Peter incredulously blurts out, "You do? I hope it's a boy!" No sooner did the words spill from his mouth than he realizes his mistake.

Bael looks back and forth between the two and says, "I have a son, but he was taken from me when he was just an infant. It is still very, very painful. I'd rather not talk about it if you don't mind."

The Portly Lady returns her gaze to Bael. "Of course! This donation is so exceedingly kind of you," as she shoves the money in her expensive trench coat. "These kids always need someone to look out for them. *Believe—you—me*," she says in an exaggerated tone as she throws her hands to her well-padded hips and says, "It's so important to have a positive male influence these days. Exactly how many farmhands were you thinking about? We can certainly stand to lighten the load. Maybe a dozen or so?" she asks as she throws her arms open.

He looks at her without saying a word.

"What was I thinking? Farms take a lot of work, especially if you want to use child labor so you can pocket most of the money yourself," she says with a wink. "Would you rather two dozen? Of course, there would be a small matter of the fee."

"Fee?"

"Yes, think of it as a rehoming fee. Like you'd see at a pet rescue. We get them healthy, give them their shots, and then you bring them home with you. I have some brochures I could show you."

"I understand, but I'd only like to welcome three boys into our quaint little family."

She sighs and drops her shoulders. "That's it? Well, you've still come to the right place. We have plenty of boys here! Mind you, the lot of them are downright lazy, though. How about you spend some time here and watch how they do their chores. We believe a person must earn their lot in life—even if it is *just* a kid. You just watch and point a few of them out to me. I'll personally take care of the rest."

Peter says, "I think..." and Bael promptly stomps on his foot, causing him to lose his balance and stumble right into the Portly Lady. Her purse opens, and an entire roll of hundred dollar bills falls to the floor.

Peter screams, "Wow! That's a lot of money! Did you rob a bank or something?" Being the closest to the wad of cash, Peter reaches his arm out to pick it up. Somehow the plump woman standing several feet away gets to it first. Her face reddens, and she roughly shoves the money back inside her purse and zips it closed. The woman says, "Now go along. Pick out a few of them. You also let me know if you change your mind and want more than three," she says as she rubs her sausage thumb against the tips of her index and middle fingers together, making the money sign. "Now, please do come in and make yourselves right at home."

Bael says, "Thank you. Do the children live here?"

"Well, they do until I sell them off," she blushes and

clears her throat, "I mean find their forever homes."

"Well, I'd better get to it."

Bael walks into the *family room*, followed by Peter and Sully, where they see about 25 kids ranging from preteens up about 18.

Chapter 8

ZACK

Zack sits off to the side by himself, appearing to be asleep. His hoodie is draped over his face, but his eyes poke out and intently and watch Bael, Peter, and Sully as they walk in. He doesn't like to remember his early childhood. He endured so much pain; it left him forever scarred. He's created a dark place within the confines of his heart where those memories have been pushed down and locked up tight like a sealed vault. Zack's path into foster care wasn't exceptional. He wasn't abandoned on some doorstep with a note saying, *"return to sender."* He wasn't pulled out of his mother's hysterical arms by authorities who knew how to parent him better than she could. Instead, he was loved and cherished beyond words.

The sound of trickling water still brings him back to when he rode high atop his father's broad shoulders as they skipped rocks at the local creek. The feeling of butterflies beating inside his tiny chest reminds him of when his mother would gingerly push him on the playground swings and give him butterfly kisses before bed.

His love turned to rage the day they were taken from him when he was just five. Zack had begged to go to the local toy shop, so the family loaded into the car and off they went. A teenage girl on a cell phone missed the stop sign and drove head-on into their car. His parents were killed instantly—but not him. Eight years later, he still struggles with being the sole survivor of his family. What a cruel fate to be left in this world all alone.

Gone were the days he would get along with adults and other kids or even care about what they thought of him. Although he is exceptionally bright, school is nothing more than a means to an end. It gets him away from the group home and those wretched staff for a consistent seven hours each day. Longer if he took his time getting *"home."* He could simply never return, and the group home staff would be none the wiser. It wouldn't be until the school came sniffing around the group home looking for him that they would even know he was gone.

Nobody would ever care about him like his parents had. Now, his deepest and most desperate wish is for the sweet bliss of ignorance. The ignorance to believe that his best days are yet to come. That he can truly be anything in life he wants to be if he works hard enough. No, he knows better. He's akin to an old dog at the pound. Families come in and gawk over the puppies, but the older dogs who had experienced the scars of life are ignored. Invisible. Left behind. Abandoned. Of course, this knowledge is sharpened like the blade of a knife by the cruel group home staff.

"Once you turn 18, you're OUT OF HERE! You'll be

tossed out like the trash with just the clothes on your back. And you'll count yourself lucky if I don't charge you for that!" says the Portly Lady at every turn.

Chapter 9

HUXLEY

Huxley had tucked himself in the small, open space behind a tattered up old couch. His sunken eyes blink softly as he watches the visitors enter the room. He feels like the seeds of a dandelion blowing in a gentle breeze. Its seeds spread by the smallest of life forces. Although this image seems relaxing to most people, it wouldn't feel that way if you were the dandelion who's lived your entire life being one way, then turning into something else entirely until you are a shriveled up shadow and glory of your former self. And if that's not bad enough, your pieces are taken one by one until you are left completely and utterly all alone in the world.

His parents had abandoned him before he was even old enough to realize it, but his amazing maternal grandparents picked him up once his parents had put him down, so to speak. His grandparents liked to say he was the son they never had. That God himself blessed them with someone else to love, honor, and cherish, just like in the wedding vows. Unfortunately, the very next part is *until death do you part.*

His grandmother was the first to die when Huxley was just six. His grandfather, unable to cope with her being gone, gave up the will to live just three short weeks later. They left him a generous inheritance that was enough to care for him through adulthood, which enticed his parents to rush to his side with promises of living together as a proper family. He thought visiting an attorney's office to make his parents responsible for him seemed perfectly reasonable at the time. Once they had control of the inheritance, however, they abandoned him at the group home.

By luck, he had managed to grab his one true treasure before he was forced into the car—a teddy bear from his grandparents named Wally. His grandmother had used his old baby blanket to hand-stitch a shirt for the brown bear. For weeks he sat in the corner and clung to the bear with tears running down his face. Those people who would tell you to stand up to bullies never had to live here. The older boys grabbed his tattered old bear and animatedly tossed it back and forth over his head in a sort of monkey-in-the-middle game. They taunted him to try and get it back. When he reacted, they hit and kicked him until he had no further fight left in him.

They forced him to watch as they used the bear in a tug-of-war match and ripped it beyond repair. When he later tried to get food at the table, they took immense pleasure in taking that from him, too.

His overly thin arms and legs show a pattern of old scars, along with plenty of new ones. The group home staff tell others that he's so skinny because he chooses not to eat what's served. Anyone with a heart would be able to see how frightened he is to get too close to the table while others are there. He learned to stay in the corner—trying to be invisible—only coming out when it's *safe*.

Chapter 10

OMAR

Omar sits like a king as he punches one large fist into the other. He was abandoned at the hospital when he was born. He never knew his parents—or for that matter even their names. His mother walked right out of the hospital after giving birth to him. Like the hospital was nothing more than a drive-through delivery stop. She used a fake name, so she knew that she wanted nothing to do with him from the beginning. Does he have siblings? Aunts? Uncles? Grandparents?

His name was "Baby Boy" for the first year of his life until a social worker finally named him Omar—meaning *one who flourishes*. He was placed in a series of foster homes along the way, never learning how to bond with people, including other children. Like baby songbirds, they must learn to sing at a critical point during their development or never will. So, too, was Omar's ability to bond with others—it was never learned.

He wasn't held, nurtured, or loved. His boo boos were never kissed. He didn't have someone waiting with a band-aid. His nightmares were both at night and during the day. In a foster home setting, that meant not getting along with his foster parents' biological children. So, after being physically and verbally aggressive, he bounced around from home to home. When he learned to target his rage on other foster children and not the biological children, there wasn't a foster family around town that didn't know his reputation.

He is the biggest and oldest child at the group home. He's also its resident bully. The group home staff use him to help keep order and control of the children. In exchange for *helping* the staff, he receives his own bed and extra food. However, the big oaf is too dumb to know that every child there would rather sleep in a bathtub filled with ice than to share a bed with him. He's also big enough to take all the food he wants anyway.

He forces the children to complete all the household chores—and then some—some that make absolutely no sense at all. Things like answering the phone and taking food service orders. Using their already limited food supply, he forces the orphans to make and deliver takeout orders. The Portly Lady uses their food budget to buy sandwich meat and bread in bulk from the local box shop.

Through an extensive word of mouth network around town, people knew to call in their sandwich orders for free delivery. Her mark-up costs for the sandwiches are relatively high for the area, intended to discourage customers from leaving the orphans a delivery tip— instead of choosing to spend all their money on the food itself—lining the Portlady Lady's sticky pockets. It wasn't all in vain, though. She was exceptionally generous in sharing the stale bread and expired meat with the children. They could always count on limitless gristle—the part of the flesh that most people cut off or politely spit into their napkins.

The orphans expertly prepare a variety of sandwiches like triple-decker club sandwiches, pastrami on rye, French dips with au jus, Rueben sandwiches, patty melts, and meatball subs. Unbeknownst to the children, the more they try to please the Portly Lady with their cooking and delivery skills, the more likely she is to sabotage potential adoptions.

"Ouch!" cries a small child falling to his knees as Omar grabs his ear and twists.

"You need to deliver this to 108 Smith Street. Don't come back without the money! Do you understand what I'll do to you if you make me mad?"

"Y-y-yes."

"GO!"

WHACK! He smacks a six-year-old across the face for not mopping the floors fast enough. *CLASH!* He bangs two pot lids in another child's ears for having to be told to take out the trash.

Bael watches the scene unfolding before him. He does a quick nod of his head and pulls Peter aside. "Do you remember what we talked about?"

"Yeah, yeah. School, farm, father, and..."

"NO! That's—not—what—I'm—talking—about! I need you to speak to those three children," Bael motions to Zack, Omar, and Huxley. "I need you to convince those boys to come with us. Remember, they must tell me that they will come *freely.*"

Peter tilts his head. "That *freely* thingy is important to you, isn't it?"

"It's more important than you realize."

"Okay, so tell me."

"It's the key to my energy source and soon to be yours, too."

"What happens if they don't agree to go with you freely?"

"Well, if *I* ask them and they say no, then they will pull from my life source instead of me pulling from theirs."

"Oh! So, is that why you want me to ask them?"

"Yes!"

"Are you trying to off me or something?"

"No, silly child. It's still safe for you right now if they say no."

"So, there will come a time?"

"Yes."

"See! I told you that I could be the brains behind this operation! I've got this! But seriously, why those three? I can pick out three better ones."

"Peter, do you understand me?"

"Fine, fine. Don't blow a gasket!"

Chapter 11

Peter watches Zack pass through the back door. He turns to Bael and says, "I've got this. Come on, Sully."

"Okay, just like we talked about it."

"Remember, I'm the brains behind this operation."

And in nearly one fluid motion, Peter reaches his hand into the backpack of one of the foster kids and swipes a baseball and heads for the back door. The door is missing a doorknob and falls off one of its hinges as he pushes on it. Holding up the door, he calls for Sully to pass through. Once they're both out, he slams his back into the door, trying to force it back into place, which proves to be mildly successful. Zack didn't seem to have this much trouble as he passed through.

Once he finally fights his way out the door, Peter tosses the dirty ball up in the air several times, teasing the dog and getting him excited. He then throws the ball against the retention wall THUD— THUD —THUD. The wall is unevenly constructed of various-sized rocks, looking much like the crooked writing on an unlined scrap of paper. It starts off high and ever so slowly falls lower and lower. A variety of wildly growing red, pink, and purple ornamental cabbage litter the cracks and crevices.

During the heat of the afternoon sun, black and yellow garter snakes with a kiss of red pop their creepy heads out and offer an enchanting hiss. Sully frantically chases the ball with his jowls flapping in the wind as he throws himself up into the air and does a whole-body contortion trying to catch the ball. Out of the corner of his eye, Peter notices Zack rubbernecking them as the ball bounces wildly between them. *Bingo!*

Sensing the time is ripe with possibilities, he says, "Hey, I'm Peter." Pointing his thumb in the dog's direction, "This is Sully."

"I'm Zack. Hey, um do you think your dog would do that for me?"

"What? Look dumb?"

"No, I mean chase the ball."

He lets out a snort and says, "He's a nut. Why don't you give it a go?"

Zack eagerly picks up the soggy ball and throws it against the wall—saliva shoots out from the ball in every direction. Sully excitedly runs after it, exactly like he had with Peter.

"Hey, look! He likes you! He doesn't like just everyone. He must see something special in *you*."

Zack mutters under his breath, "Nobody—EVER—sees—anything—special—in—me."

Lowering his head, "I know just how you feel. I know what it's like not to have a home." Zack says nothing, but Peter knows he's listening. "I was all alone in the world, except for this goofy dog. Before Bael, that is. He *saved* me."

"Really?"

"Yeah, really. It's great. For the first time, I feel like, well, like I belong. Like we've just always known each other. I do have one complaint, though."

"I figured as much. Nothing is ever what it seems. I've learned that over and over again. What is it?"

"He does make me go to school, though. Ugh, he goes on and on about how important it is to have a future. Blah, blah, blah! Imagine that! I guess I really shouldn't complain, though. It's nice having someone who cares enough about me to worry about my future."

"That's not bad at all. If you don't mind me saying so, you two look an awful lot alike. If you didn't tell me you were adopted, well, I would have thought that he was your real dad."

"That's interesting." He pauses. "Anyway, Bael says you can come with us, too. Of course, you'd have to go to school, work hard, try your best. Blah! Blah! Blah! Do you want that? I guess that would make us—well, it would make us brothers. Sully would love that, too. We'd be a family."

Zack's voice goes up several octaves and he blurts out, "I'd love to have a family again and a dog. Yes!"

"Okay, but Bael needs to hear you say that you want to go with us *freely*. He wants to make sure he's not pressuring you or anything. He says adults always force kids to do stuff they don't want to do just because they're kids. He doesn't want to do the same thing."

Rolling his eyes, he says, "Yeah, isn't that the truth!"

"Can you do that? Can you tell him you choose to go

freely with us?"

"I sure can. Let's go do it NOW! I want out of this rat hole!"

Zack abandons the gooey ball in the mound of dirt known as the backyard. Sully spots it, lets out a playful bark, and pounces right on top of it like a linebacker. But just as fast, he drops it out of his wide-open mouth when he realizes that no one is there to throw it for him.

Peter and Zack sprint around the perimeter of the house looking for Bael—then barrel through the front door, nearly tripping over each other as they stop on a dime. He and the Portly Lady are talking in hushed voices in her office, hunkered over some sort of map. Hearing the door slam and impending pile-up, Bael turns around and spies the two boys.

Looking first annoyed and then pleased, he winks his eye and says, "Excuse me, kind lady." Turning to the boys, he says, "Let's go outside, shall we? It's such a lovely day after all. There's not a cloud in the sky."

They walk outside and stop at the base of the worn steps. Peter bounces on his feet as Zack draws alternating circles in the dirt with his tattered sneakers.

"Bael, Zack wants to join us. Go ahead, Zack, tell him."

Pausing, he stutters, "Yeah, um, what Peter, uh, said," says Zack.

Bael says, "Zack, I need to hear it from you."

Looking completely interested in his feet, he says, "Yeah."

"Can you say that you agree to come with me freely, please? If you don't mind, I'm just going to take your hands for a moment."

Taking a step back, he says, "Um, I'm not sure about

that."

"About going with us?"

"No, I'm just not sure I want you touching me."

"I'm sorry, Zack, but I must insist."

"Ugh, okay then. If you have to."

Bael grasps Zack's hands. "Go ahead and say it, Zack."

Still gazing down intently at his feet, he says, "I agree to go with you freely."

"That was good, Zack. But can you look me in the eyes and say that?"

Bringing his distrustful eyes up to meet Bael's, he says the oath. From the crooked wooden bench, Peter keenly watches their entire conversation. With a lifeforce all their own, his own eyes feel like the soft humming and throbbing of a dull headache, pulsating as he watches what's unfolding right before him. His attention falters when his hyper-focused eyes alert him to the Portly Lady watching from her office. *Weird.* Her eyes had shown the same blue as Bael's eyes. *Why hadn't he noticed that before?*

Meanwhile, fallen leaves are picked up in a rush of wind that takes Peter's breath away. Immediately, Zack strugges as he tries to pull his hands free from Bael.

Zack's panicked face cries out, "It—feels—like—fire—in—my—veins! LET—GO!" His eyes had started off with the eagerness of a child on Christmas morning, then quickly transform into the discovery of a real-life boogeyman living under your bed. The leaves rustle about, but fall short of breaking the invisible barrier of a near-perfect circle surrounding the two of them. A loud hum like the sound of an electrical transformer envelopes them.

Zack cries out, "Hey, what—is—that? What—are—

you—doing—to—me?"

After what feels like several minutes had passed, Bael releases Zack's hands and gingerly responds, "That, dear Zack, is your new family connection. We are linked together for life now."

Violently rubbing his hands, he asks, "So, what does that mean exactly?"

"It means that you will never leave me."

Beads of sweat connect and roll down Zack's forehead, leaving dime-sized circles on the ground.

"And—and what would happen if I ever left?"

"That, dear Zack, would be a fate far worse than death. But alas, that is no way to celebrate your special day as you join our family."

"Are—you—threatening—me?"

"I do not need to threaten anyone. *It simply is.* You can go pack your personal belongings now because we'll be leaving soon."

"Well, you're looking at it. I don't have anything. The Portly Lady might even charge you for the clothes I'm wearing," Zack says, motioning with the back of his hand from head to toe. "Although they did buy them with the money that was given to them about ten years ago—originally for a different kid. She keeps passing them down and lining her pockets with the money she saves. She won't be happy."

"The Portly Lady and I go way back. We share some—*commonalities.* You can go and play ball, and I'll let you know when we're ready to leave."

Zack doesn't waste any time and runs away. Peter turns to Bael and exclaims, "HEY, I could feel my eyes pulsating when you did the ritual with Zack. Is that normal?"

"That is excellent, Peter! Do you want to take part in the next one? I think you're ready now."

"Would I ever!"

Chapter 12

Peter strides around the perimeter of the house for the tallest kid. He doesn't see him, so he goes to Omar's second most frequented spot: the kitchen. There are a dozen young children there prepping for the day's take-out menu.

Peter's eyes go wide and he asks, "What are you all doing?"

The tweens look up at him, then hang their heads and continue working. One child is preparing oven-baked meats. One is basting them. One is slicing the cheese on the deli slicer. Two are kneading the bread dough. Two are hand slicing potatoes into small slivers for yet another to hand-fry into freshly made potato chips. One is on the phone taking call-in orders and writing them down. Another is sitting at the desk and retrieving fax and email orders. Two are tasked with getting any necessary supplies and ingredient refills. Judging by the bushels of cucumbers, pickling spices, and canning jars that are being retrieved, the group will be making homemade pickles next.

Peter grabs two slices of cheese from the stack of newly sliced American cheese and asks, "So how often does the Department of Health inspect this place?" When no one answers him, "Cat got your tongues? No bother, you'd probably just fry them up with the potato chips anyway!" He chuckles and continues his search.

He walks over to the second-floor staircase, looks up, and shakes his head in disbelief. Afraid he might plunge through the rotting wooden steps, he carefully extends one foot at a time in front of him and gently touches every step before placing his full weight on them. Once he's safely on the second floor, he investigates the two bedrooms. One room has several children who are barely in their double-digits, bottle-feeding five infants. The other room has still yet more kids feeding jars of pureed food to more babies.

"So out of curiosity," he asks the tweens in the second room, "who makes that food?"

A timid little child replies, "The kitchen staff."

"And by the staff, you mean the kids, right?"

She hangs her head down.

"Doesn't the government or anybody check in on this place?"

A girl with long, raggedy hair wearing tattered clothes looks into his eyes.

"Well, answer me!"

Looking like it was connected to a lever and pulley, the girl's head lifts. She says blankly, "The babies don't stay here that long. She sells them."

Peter's mouth drops, but not at her answer. But because she answered his question when she looked into his eyes. He replies, "Well, I guess they must not care what goes on here. No bother."

He walks out of the room and expects to find more hazardous stairs to climb, but that would have been preferential to what he sees in their absence. The third-floor bedroom is an attic. It's accessed by pulling down a ladder and entering through the loft hatch door. He climbs up the steps and stops midway to use his teeth to pull out a splinter from his hand. Turning his head to the side, he spits it out—some spittle dribbles down his chin. The smell of dirty diapers slaps him hard across the face, and he vomits a little in his mouth. He pulls himself up and flops onto the landing above just like a flounder.

The room is a large loft on the underside belly of the pitched roof. There are exposed nails coming through the ceiling. The long, wooden rafters that supply support to the weather-damaged roof are beginning to separate. It's just a matter of time until the entire thing collapses. The darkened room does not have any windows, and the single light hanging from one of the rafters casts creepy shadows throughout the room. Holding up his hands, Peter casts an alligator shadow puppet on the far wall.

Chuckling, Peter says, "Don't be sad you don't have any windows. Those holes in the walls are all you *really* need."

Several tweens are sitting on the mattresses changing baby diapers like they're on a conveyer belt. Once a dirty diaper is removed, it is balled up and thrown to another child standing beside the wall. Four open garbage bags are lining the walls loaded with dirty, poopy diapers. Flies are buzzing around the bags like they're on a picnic. A diaper is tossed over Peter's head, and he looks up just in time for some droplets of urine to land on his forehead.

"UGH! You people are animals!"

He looks around, but Omar isn't here, either. Unable to resist, he asks, "Hey, how do you carry the babies upstairs? Do you climb with one hand and hold the baby with the other? Or do you just toss them up, and someone catches them? I guess it really wouldn't matter if you dropped one because there's probably someone at the door right now dropping off a new one. You know what they say, when one door closes, another opens!"

The tweens do not answer him, and he climbs back down the ladder. "Hey up there, I feel like Donkey Kong!"

Peter carefully climbs down the stairs and returns to the first floor. Where else could this big oaf be? He's about to ask one of the staff when he hears some rumbling from the coat closet near the Porty Lady's office. Peter quietly opens the door and finds Omar in there, teasing one of the younger children. He looks like a professional football player taunting a player on the peewee flag football team. The child begins to cry, which fuels Omar's taunts.

Omar sings in a baratone voice, "Cry baby, cry baby, little orphan blue. Go tell some—one who cares about you! Oh, wait! You're here. Nobody does care about YOU!"

Peter looks at both children and throws his palms up. Does he even realize the irony in his song? But sticking with the plan, he lets out an evil-sounding shrill and plucks a rock that was lodged in the tread of his shoe, then throws it at the small boy. "Hey, I think that the *BABY* just wet his pants! Quick, does anyone have a d-d-diaper!"

Omar looks over at Peter—at once round housing his brutish force in Peter's direction. He looks him up and down as he smacks his fist into his hand.

"HEY, YOU GOTTA PROBLEM OR SOMETHIN'?"

He yawns and says, "No, my name is Peter. Hey, did you come up with that song on your own? I like it! That stupid crybaby! How can you even take it here?"

The obtuse oaf smiles. "Yeah, I made it up. I hate these sniffling, sneezing crybabies. I can't take it no more!"

"What if I tell you that you can leave these crybabies behind?"

"Um. I don't get it. Like put 'em behind me?"

"Dude, I mean that you can leave this place in the dust." He watches Omar's head tilt to the side like Sully's does.

"You gonna make 'em clean the dust? They already do that."

"Okay, I mean do you want to go out and have some real fun? Do what you want—when you want. No rules."

"Yeah, right! Who's gonna make the take-out orders?"

"What's up with that, anyway? This isn't how I expected a foster home to be."

"The Portly Lady takes care of stuff. Don't ask no more questions."

"Yeah, whatever. Hey, that guy that I'm with, Bael, well, he adopted me when nobody else wanted me. Now I get to do what I want—when I want—however I want to do it. I don't have any dumb staff lecturing me. I don't have to go to school. Do this—oh, don't do that—blah, blah, blah!"

"What's the catch?"

"There's no catch. You just have to tell Bael that you want to go with us *freely*. He's not one to tell kids what to do. He's afraid that we'll grow up and pummel him if he makes us mad. Besides, I need someone to have some fun with. We can be partners in crime!"

"Um, cool! Wanna rob a bank?"

"Maybe later...but if you want to go, you have to tell Bael first."

"If you're lying to me, I'm gonna," he says as he punches his meaty fist into his open palm.

Answering dryly, "Yes, I'm shaking." Lifting his voice, he continues saying, "But anyway, you'll have to tell him."

"I'll give him a knuckle sandwich too if he's lying to me."

Peter flashes a dramatic expression on his face and says, "Let's go tell him."

The two find Bael sitting outside on the front steps of the rickety old front porch. "Hey, Bael. Omar says he wants to go with us. Isn't that cool?"

Bael turns to Omar, "Did Peter tell you I don't like to boss kids around?"

"Yeah," says Omar. "He also said you're afraid of us," Omar says as he punches his fist again.

Bael casts a quick look at Peter and raises his eyebrows. He says wryly, "Terrified. Well, I need to hear you tell me that you want to go with us freely. That way, I know you feel okay going with us. Okay?"

"Yeah."

"Do you mind if we take your hands as you tell us?"

"Um, where you gonna take 'em?"

"I meant, do you mind if I hold your hands?"

"Yeah."

Peter assumes he means *yeah you can* and not *yeah I mind.* Bael must think the same thing because he takes hold of one of Omar's sweaty hands and instructs Peter to take the other, shooting a *don't even think of fighting me* look at him. Then Bael and Peter finish off the triangle by grasping their remaining two hands together. The air around them stirs. Leaves jump up and dance around them like happy little ballerinas, then take on the anger of mother nature during a tornado.

Bael and Peter's eyes both pulsate brilliant blue as Bael feeds the oath one word at a time to Omar. A forcefield wraps around the three of them like a deep crimson electric lasso with brilliant bright white sparks shooting out in every direction.

Peter looks over his shoulder. Just like with Zack, the Portly Lady watches from her office window. Her eyes are aglow in brilliant blue and transfixed on the trio.

Dropping Peter's and Omar's hands, Bael says to Omar, "Now we're a family. You're a part of me, and I'm a part of you—never to be separated."

Omar says, "Cool," then turns to Peter and whispers, "What does *freely* mean? Am I going to have to pay for something?"

Bael commands, "Go back inside, Omar."

"The house?"

"Yes, the house."

Peter turns to Bael, "Hey, do you know that the Portly Lady is watching us?"

"What do you mean?" asks Bael.

"Well, she watched when you worked your magic on Zack, and again with the dumb oaf."

"You noticed that."

"Yes. Why?"

"She is like us, Peter. Did you notice her eyes?"

"Yeah. They looked hypnotizing, just like yours."

"Like yours now, too."

"Really?"

"Yes."

"Does she feed off these kids?"

"Yes. She is extremely powerful."

"Is that why she's so fat?"

Laughing, "Well, she also enjoys human food."

"Judging by her size, I'd say she more than enjoys it. And is that why this place looks like a human landfill? Is it because she has the power to run this place any way she wants to?"

"Yes, yes it is."

Chapter 13

Peter sets off to find Huxley. He's a scrawny child with no real predictable hiding place other than being away from others who wish to cause him pain—so that's a tough find at the foster home. Peter is reluctant to go upstairs. Afraid the manservant Lurch from the Addams Family will open the staircase, releasing a cloud of smoke and bellow out in his baritone voice, *"You rang..."*

Peter expects to find Huxley working like a house-elf in the kitchen as he slaves away for the Portly Lady's thriving take-out business, but Huxley isn't there either. He walks around to the outside of the dilapidated old house. A flood of tears streams down Huxley's dirty face revealing clusters of freckles. Peter silently watches as Huxley carefully unties the bags one at a time. He submerges his hands into the bags and extracts scraps of bread and mystery meat—Reminding Peter of the Kevin Costner movie *Waterworld*. In that movie, drinking water was in such short supply that the main character filtered and drank his own urine. Huxley rolls the food into a ball and pushes it into his mouth. He swallows hard, but it looks like it's stuck in his throat like an Adam's apple. Huxley's body begins to wretch, and he vomits the ball onto the ground like a furball entwined with sticky saliva.

GROWL. Peter can hear Huxley's overly convex stomach growling like a grizzly bear from several feet away. His shoulders look like they will swallow his neck whole if he isn't careful. His sad, brown eyes communicate it all. Peter leans against the house, putting one foot up against the wooden exterior, careful to avoid the ball of vomit. Looking down, he shivers as he spies a large spider crawling over his exposed ankle.

Crackle. Peter slowly opens a Twinkie. "This is *de—li—cious!*"

Huxley looks at the Twinkie like a shark smelling blood in the water.

In a soothing sing-song voice, Peter asks, "Dude, have you ever had one of these?"

Softly, he replies, "No."

"Would you *LIKE* to have one?"

"Really? W-w-why would y-y-you give *me* one?"

"It's no problem. I have extras. Here you go."

With shaking hands, Huxley slowly takes the Twinkie from Peter's outstretched hand. He hides it in his hand and quickly looks around—his eyes squinting as he waits. And waits. And waits. Then he feverishly turns his body around. The bruises on his tiny arms are shadowed by dirt, causing him to blend in like a chameleon. In one fluid motion, he unwraps it with his dirty little hands and stuffs the entire thing into his mouth like a chipmunk. The white cream oozes out of the sides of his mouth like a popped zit.

"There's more of where that came from, little buddy. All the food you can eat. Candy, cupcakes, cookies. Hey, all those foods begin with the letter C. Don't worry, you can eat foods that start with other letters, too!" he chuckles.

"You just have to tell my adopted dad that you choose to come *freely* with us. He doesn't want to force kids to go with him. He knows that kids like us are bullied into doing things, and he doesn't want to do the same thing. But if you'd rather stay here..."

Through his stuffed cheeks, Huxley mumbles something unintelligible. He takes off in a sprint with his neck flailing about like a rubber chicken. Peter is out of breath as he takes off in a sprint after him. When Peter finally catches up to him, Huxley had already found Bael, who is tapping his foot impatiently.

"Now that we're all here—Huxley, if you don't mind, please hold Peter's hands."

He eagerly extends his hands to Peter. "I-I-I want to go w-w-with you!"

"I do apologize if this sounds bossy, but for my peace of mind, I'd like to hear you say that you choose to go with Peter freely. Okay?"

With tightly grasped hands, Huxley excitedly says, "Yes, yes I choose to go with you freely!"

"Nice job, Huxley, but can you please say that you choose to go freely *with Peter*?"

"Yes! I choose to go with freely with Peter."

As he lets out the final word of the oath, the same crimson glow surrounds the three of them. The same bright white sparks fly out in every direction like a sparkler. Peter is still expending the same amount of force as he holds Huxley's hands—but suddenly, Huxley cries out in pain. His mouth is ajar as he looks at Peter's hands that are now crushing his like a vice grip.

Once Peter no longer sees the crimson rain surrounding them, he releases Huxley's hands. The poor boy's jagged fingernails are etched into the side of his hands, tearing apart his flesh. His tear-stained face is once again wet. He blows on his hands and quickly scurries away, leaving little droplets of red in his wake.

Peter's face grimaces. But Bael says proudly, "Don't worry, he *can't* go far. I can feel your power getting stronger, Peter. I'm so proud of you!"

"Why is that woman still watching us?"

"Peter, every time we take someone's life force, we *all* get stronger—the power it yields can be felt the world over."

"So, I?"

"Yes."

Chapter 14

Bael glances up as the tick, tick, ticking of the clock seems to be slowing down as if he's trying to watch a freshly painted portrait dry. He pushes the shabby, mismatched curtains aside and looks out the window several times. As the curtains fall back down, a cloud of dust obscures the high noon sun. As he presses his back against the wall, several brown cockroaches scurry for safety, each going in different directions. One crawls right up the Portly Lady's exposed leg, onto her ruffled red skirt, over her torso, and down her chubby arm and directly into the center of her triple-decker turkey and bacon club sandwich with globs of mayonnaise oozing from the sides.

Bael announces, "My dear staff, I regret to inform you that we must be leaving this afternoon."

"Oh, codswallop!" says the Portly Lady with disappointment filling her round face. Emotionally taking another large bite of her sandwich, a soft crunch of exoskeleton crackles in her mouth. I already tossed those worthless kids out into the backyard to sleep under the trees. You, Peter, and Sully can have their blankets, pillows, and bedroom for as long as you'd like. Between us, it's nice to have someone else to talk to other than these brats," lowering her voice with her wrinkled hand cupped over the side of her large mouth, "and this useless staff. Besides, I thought you were staying through the weekend."

"I am quite disappointed to leave, but the farm animals need tending to. I have cows, pigs, sheep, and a wonkey little donkey named Bartholomule."

"What kind of name is that?" asks Peter.

Bael looks crossly at him, and Peter theatrically twists his lips like he's locking them and tosses the key over the back of his shoulder.

Several staff members slowly inch within earshot. "Mr. Bael, I understand. However, we always ask our adoptive parents to have a home study. We need references. We must go to court and tell a judge that the children should go with you. That sort of thing." She throws her hand up to cup her mouth again, then lowers her voice and says, "But if you ask me, it's all just a bunch of needless rigamarole. If someone is willing to take them, they should just go. Fewer mouths to feed."

"I understand. I do apologize, but I really must be going *today*. I'm afraid I simply cannot wait. I have already been gone for far too long as it is. If the boys don't come with me, I simply cannot come back and get them. Surely you understand the hard life of a simple farmer. But, if you simply must, I'm sure you will be able to line up other adoptive parents for three older boys. I bet people must be lining up to help make a difference in the life of one of these teens. Naturally, I would be deeply disappointed."

"I could put an ad in the Sunday newspaper advertising a dozen for one sale, and STILL no one would want them. I give up my valuable time to come and tend to them. Mind you, do you think I ever get a thank you?"

Peter turns to Bael and whispers, "Yeah, isn't that kind of her *job*? Doesn't she get paid to be here? Besides, she looks like she collects her paycheck five times over with all the food she stuffs in her..."

With one fluid motion, Bael shimmies up to Peter and stomps on his left foot, landing squarely on his little pinky toe. Peter lets out a cry, doubles over, and promptly shuts up.

The Portly Lady says, "Let's not be hasty here. Since you've already been through the adoption process with Peter, we can just *enhance* the paperwork. I trust everything is just as you say it is."

He grasps her right hand like a gentleman, places his left hand behind his back, bows deeply, and pronounces, "Kind woman, everything is most certainly as I described it to be. My only concern is being able to enroll the boys in school. Would you be ever so kind as to mail me the papers so I can enroll them as soon as possible?"

"See! That just proves they should leave with you TODAY! That's simply perfect!"

Peter shifts back and forth on his feet, then blurts out to Bael, "Yeah, that and the fact that you paid her off!"

Pretending like she didn't hear him, the Portly Lady snaps her bulbous fingers at two small children—dirty little waifs sitting in the corner trying desperately to blend in as they await her latest marching orders.

In a shrill voice, "You two," she snaps her fingers in

their faces, "make sandwiches for their long journey to the *farm*. Don't waste the good stuff on the foster kids. You know what to do."

"Yes, ma'am!" they say in unison. They quickly dash for the kitchen, careful to avoid Omar. They prepare ham, cheese, and bacon sandwiches on fluffy homemade white bread for Bael and Peter. Sully—a juicy bone with chunks of meaty flesh still clinging to it. Zack, Huxley, and Omar have mustard sandwiches on stale, week-old bread. They place the sandwiches into a paper bag and hand it to the Portlady Lady for inspection. She takes out the two ham and cheese sandwiches, unwraps one, and slides out a piece of the bacon. Turning her head, she pushes the entire slice into her mouth. To Sully's delight, flake-sized crumbles fall to the floor. Next, she opens the three cheese and mustard sandwiches. She counts two slices of cheese on each sandwich and pulls the sandwich makers aside.

"You ungrateful little brats! You know that you are only to put one slice of cheese on each sandwich. That's going to cost each of you tonight's dinner to make up for it."

She continues looking through the bag and a look of disappointment captures her face as she stares at the juicy meat bone that otherwise would have been sold to the local dog food company. Last, there are water bottles for each of them.

The Portlady Lady announces, "Bael, Peter, and Sully can each have a water bottle. The others can drink pond water for all I care." And she removes three of the waters.

The foster home staff says their goodbyes to Bael, Peter, and Sully. Rounding on Omar, Huxley, and Zack— the Portly Lady, followed by her entourage, say in hushed voices, "Don't you three mess this up. You're lucky to even leave here with the clothes on your back. Don't you make me regret this. If he brings you back here, we'll make you PAY!"

Zack scrunches his nose, lowers his thick eyebrows, and contemptuously whispers to her, "You should be happy. You're getting rid of three kids who know your secrets. Those things you try to hide from the State on the rare occasion when they come here and check on us. Yeah, those secrets that I have kept to myself until *just the right time*."

The Portly Lady's eyes bulge, and she begins to choke on her own saliva. Once her coughing fit subsides, she says, "You boys just run along now. You can keep the clothes you're wearing. Consider it a present from Auntie Claudia!"

Zack tilts his head and looks around. "Who's Auntie Claudia?"

The Portly Lady chuckles. "You've always been a funny one, Zeek! You know that's me! Now run along before it gets dark. Kisses!"

Omar turns to Zack and Huxley and asks, "How can she make us pay? We don't even have jobs."

They leave the group home and walk outside in the afternoon sun. The autumn air has a refreshing crisp to it. The deciduous leaves have started to transform Mother Nature's beauty into brilliant hues of red, orange, and gold. Sully passes the time by chasing the slowly gliding leaves as they lazily fall one by one from trees that no longer have any use for them.

Peter glances back at the three orphans trailing behind them and asks Bael, "Hey, so why did you pick THAT place?"

"I've been there before."

"Did you get kids like this before?"

"In a sense."

"What happened to them?"

"One of them you currently call dad."

Peter's eyes bulge like a bubbly-eyed goldfish. Stuttering, he asks, "Y-y-you?"

"More on that one later. But who else might you address in such a manner?"

"Tom? But how do you know him?"

"Well, we both were in the same foster home. In fact, we were at THAT very one. Sadly, it looked then much like it does now. Always an embarrassment for me. The same muddled yard, dilapidated roof, windows with baseball-sized holes in them never to be repaired. I watched others with so much less potential get adopted, but I was always left behind. It was then I learned to take control over my own destiny."

"Wait, I thought Tom had parents. Why was he at the foster home?"

"Let me guess, parents you've never met, right? In thirteen years, doesn't that seem a bit odd to you?"

Peter drops his mouth in stunned disbelief. "No, I've never met them. I always just assumed they hated who he married. Man, I hope you used your mind control on that big fat liar! I hope you made him do all sorts of horrible things!"

"Yes and no. I was just a kid at the time. My power had to be developed. I always knew I was different, but I didn't know just how different I really was. Do you ever feel that way?"

Smacking himself squarely on the forehead like Bael just hit the nail on the head, "All— the—time!"

"I had to harness my powers. Tom and I spent a lot of time together. At one point, I even considered him to be my best friend. I sort of practiced on him. When I became stronger, he turned against me."

"That two-faced traitor! I *really* need to help you to be a better judge of character!"

Not hiding a chuckle, Bael lets out, "Indeed! Well, Tom began to despise me for my power. He began to argue with me constantly. He tried to abandon me just like my parents had.

He learned how to pull on my special powers. How to drain me like a treacherous leach. He even managed to tap into some of my mind control powers. He harnessed my power and saved it until prospective adoptive parents came sniffing around. I had wondered why he was dressed up in his Sunday best. Mind you; you see how the foster kids dress. That wasn't saying much, but I did notice it all the same. It was then that he took the opportunity to abandon me.

But he did not have the happy ending he thought he would have. Once he was away from me, he could no longer use my power on his adoptive parents. They saw right through him and quickly kicked him out. He came straight back here. Right—back—to—me. Just like I knew he would. But by that time, I was stronger. More confident. More in control of myself."

"Did you two become friends again?"

"Not a chance! I kept to myself, not knowing who to trust. I eventually turned 18 and was tossed out with nothing more than the clothes on my back."

"Where did you go?"

"I didn't have anywhere to go. I slept on park benches in the pitch-black darkness for a while. Much like Huxley, I was forced to pick through garbage cans for leftover scraps of food."

"No way! You and that waif have something in common!"

"Peter!"

"Yeah, yeah. Go ahead, Hux Senior!"

"I decided to take responsibility for myself and my future. I got a job at the local grocery store. I worked hard and was able to start taking care of myself. I eventually met a young woman who frequented the store."

"Ugh! I don't know what's worse, that you met a woman or that you have something in common with Hux Junior!"

Without missing a beat, he says, "We were married. She had long blonde hair. The bluest eyes you've ever seen. Even bluer than mine. We were married for three short years."

"What happened to her?"

"She is—*was*—Kate's sister."

"My Kate?"

"Yes."

"What happened to her?"

"We were deeply in love. She died thirteen years ago."

"How did she die?"

"That, Peter, is an especially important story. One that I can't and won't rush through. In time you will know all of the details."

"Okay, I understand your dead wife story will take a long time, but can you tell me about my grandparents? My mother's parents."

"When the time is right, you will learn that your grandparents are one in the same."

"One in the same? What does that even mean? Like, are Kate and Tom brother and sister? Am I a freak or something?"

His sudden smile betrays the serious tone of his voice. "Later. For now, your grandmother had her own set of magical powers. She used that necklace you found against me. It has immense strength and is capable of extraordinary magic."

"We have to go back and get it!"

"Indeed!"

"But how will we find it? I looked forever for it. I even checked and double-checked all her normal hiding places. I, for example, have my own extraordinary power of finding my Christmas presents."

Bael says dryly, "Charming." Returning to his normal drawl, "That necklace was used against me, but now that you and I have been reunited, our strength has been compounded. Given enough time, we should be able to find it together."

"Reunited?"

"We have found each other again."

GRRR! "Dude, I know what that prefix means!"

"Right, well we will have to come up with a plan on how to get Tom and Kate out of the house long enough for us to find it."

"Don't worry—I'll think of something. But you just said our reunification compounded your strength. What did you mean by that?"

"It means that I can do things now that I couldn't do

then."

"Like what?"

"Once you come into your full power as a dark elf, I will become the new ruler of our realm."

"See, I told you I was the brains behind this operation! But just so you know, I don't come cheap."

"Trust me, I know."

The two continue walking without uttering a word. They seem to be taking turns in a choreographed scene of the thumb and index finger under their respective chin followed by a grimace and vigorous head shaking back and forth.

Peter suddenly screams with jubilance, "I've got it! We just have to get them out of the house."

Flatly, Bael responds, "Yes, I already surmised as much." He smacks his lips and says, "You're a *terrific* help."

"Right! Okay, we know they are looking for me. We just have to make them think I've been spotted somewhere far enough away that they will go and look for me. We can watch the house until they both leave. Then we'll have enough time to go in and find the necklace."

"That might just work!"

Puffing up his chest, "Like I said, I'm the brains behind this operation."

Chapter 15

They walk parallel to the Mohawk River, which was flowing with a wild vengeance. They stop and watch as the river's lock system—a sort of water elevator for passing boats—opens its arms and allows a small speedboat to approach. The lock guard loudly sets off two long and two short blasts of his horn, causing Sully to moan like a low moose call. Once the water in the chamber is level with the water on the other side of the gate, it spreads its arms wide, and the boat drives out. Once the boat is nothing more than a tiny dot on the horizon, the boys begin playing around again. Omar shoves Huxley into Zack. Zack pushes Huxley right back at Omar. Huxley squeals like a real live monkey-in-the-middle. Repeat.

"Freshlings!" Bael mutters to himself as they pass a variety of brightly painted blue and yellow pile moors along the river. "Boys, come here for a minute. Let's have our first little family meeting. That's right—everyone take a seat."

Zack and Omar shove each other, hoping to be the first

to hurdle over the mushroom-shaped cement boat tie-offs—as if they're in a real life-or-death match of leapfrog. Huxley quickly scrambles to the first open pile moor and firmly plants himself as instructed.

"Enough! I'll fling the next one of you who leaps over a pile moor like a slingshot into the river!"

Zack and Omar at once fall into line, and each assume a seat on their make-shift stools. Peter continues to leap one more time before sashaying over to a vacant pile moor. He looks up at Bael and extends a quick little wink of his left eye. His lip pulls up on the same side he's trying to wink from, revealing more of a blink than a wink.

Sully says, "Arrroo," and buries his face in his paws.

Bael looks one at a time at them. A long and intense gaze before moving to the next. His eyes pulsate as he speaks. "You agreed to come with me freely. Understand that you must now stay with me. You may not leave unless I permit you to leave, and I do not have any intention of granting that permission. Do you understand me?"

Omar and Huxley both agree.

Zack crosses his arms and asks, "What would happen if we didn't stay with you?"

Bael rounds on him and sternly asks, "Are you planning on leaving, Zack?"

"No, but it just sounds odd the way you put it."

"You are bound to me. If you attempt to leave, you will suffer a fate worse than death."

Huxley and Omar both gulp so loudly it's hard to tell if the sounds came from them or the surrounding bullfrogs. Peter, meanwhile, grins as he watches the looks on the boys' faces.

Zack rolls his eyes and scoffs, "He's just being

dramatic."

"I invite you to try, Zack."

"So, are you giving me permission to leave?"

A look of shock erases the smirk from Peter's face. Bael responds, "No, definitely not.

But enough. There's so much you've missed out on while you were at the foster home. Would you mind if we took our time getting back to the farm?"

Omar takes the lead for the boys and asks, "Uh, why? We hittin' a bank or somethin'?"

"Lovely thought, but no. See, there's an arcade we'll be passing along the way to the farm. Do you know what that is? Have you ever been to one?"

"Dude—I know that I was at that rotten place—but whoever doesn't know what an arcade is—is just a loser!" bellows Omar.

"So, does that mean that you'd like to stop there on the way *home?*"

"Duh, is that *really* even a *question?* You know it!"

Bael asks, "Peter, Zack, Huxley—are you all okay with that? Of course, I'm sure that you're getting hungry, too. We can stop for dinner at the pizza restaurant across the street from the arcade. Their pizza is the best I've EVER had!"

With the mention of food, Huxley's face lights up like the star on top of a Christmas tree. A piece of frayed rope supports his over-sized, hand-me-down pants. His 7-button shirt that's missing three buttons falls from one side to the other, taking turns exposing his scarred and bruised little shoulders.

Zack creeps alongside Sully, not talking to the others. He tosses a tennis ball up into the air a few times, then throws it a few feet in front of him. The ball rolls on top of some fallen leaves and crackles as the dog steps on top of it. Without uttering a word, Zack uses a hand signal to command the dog to return the ball. He drops the wet ball right into Zack's outstretched hand. Zack rubs the wetness from his hand on his hoodie, and the two continue their game.

Omar turns to Peter and whispers, "Uh, dude, what's an arcade?"

Peter walks ahead and whispers to Bael, "Seriously, what do you see in that dumb oaf? He just asked me what an arcade is. And that skinny one? Well, if you ask me..."

"Which I clearly didn't."

"You didn't what?"

"I didn't ask you."

"Well, if you decide to, I think Omar has an exceedingly small brain inside his exceedingly large body. He reminds me of an alligator. Fun fact—did you know that mother alligators will care for their babies one day and then...*GULP!*...they become tomorrow's bite-sized appetizer!"

"Dark elves aren't much different."

Smiling uncomfortably, he continues, "And then there's Tiny Tim."

Clearing his throat, "Huxley."

"Yes, okay. Pee-wee Huxley. I mean—seriously—if the wind blows, *we*—meaning someone else because I'm not—will have to chase him halfway down the road just to catch him! Can you do that mind control thing on Sully to make him catch that little waif when he blows away?"

Bael grimaces and shakes his head. "No, Peter, it doesn't work on animals."

"Hmm, that's a crying shame. Why not?"

"Animals are generally the exception. In fact, they are quite adept at sensing my powers. Sully did from the other side of the mirror."

"Wow! Is that why you wanted to keep him?"

"That's enough for now. We're at the pizza restaurant. Don't tell the freshlings you've been here and to the arcade before."

"Um, okay. But why? What's the difference?"

"They can't learn too much about—us. Or where you lived. Your old house holds too much power."

The approach the restaurant, which is nestled in a strip of old, long-abandoned shops and cafés. The foot traffic is light and consists mainly of those people going to the restaurant and the arcade across the street. Often it's both. There is little else to do in the small, dying riverside community. The front of the restaurant has large, greasy windows. The sign blinks *Come on in...the pizza's fine!* They merrily enter the restaurant with Huxley leading the charge.

Zack turns towards Peter. He asks, "Have you ever been here before?"

Peter replies, "No. Why?"

"Just want to know what to expect."

Huxley exclaims, "WOW! WOW! WOW! That smell is—is—is absolutely intoxicating!"

The boy's body goes limp, and he looks like a wet noodle. He puckers his mouth several times, releasing a small dribble of pooled-up drool. As if announcing his presence, his stomach growls loudly.

The waiters and waitresses balance their trays high above their heads as they navigate the table-crammed restaurant. Some are more successful than others, if the red-speckled, pizza-stained walls are any indication.

Huxley turns to Bael, "So what do we do now? Do we have to call them on the phone to tell them what we want?"

"No, child. We will sit at a table and tell them what we want."

"Uh—o—okay."

Peter turns to Bael and asks, "Can we sit at *that* table?" as he points to one that's away from the restroom. "Too many people stuff themselves silly here. You know what they say, *whatever goes in must come out!*"

Zack says, "I think that's *whatever goes up must come down.*"

A waitress walks over and breaks up their conversation. She winks her eye and takes them to a table far away from the restroom. She is tall and thin, two traits that serve her well in the crowded restaurant. She walks them to a table that is oblong and has a red and white checkered plastic tablecloth adorning it.

Bael sits at the head of the table with Peter sitting right beside him. Huxley and Omar shuffle in beside each other. Zack removes a chair from the table, leaving a space in its wake. Sully saunters on over and plants himself squarely on the floor in the open space. The waitress pulls a pad out from her apron and asks for their food and drink orders.

The lofty waitress asks, "So, you boys having a party or something? Four very different-looking teenage boys," she says, chuckling towards Bael, "can't all be yours because..."

Bael begins to open his mouth and Peter spies movement from the side of the restaurant. A streak of black. A flash of blue. Then, just as fast, it was gone. A look of confusion consumes her face and she stops talking mid-thought. She stands there and blankly stares at Bael. She brings her index finger up to the side of her face and strokes her forehead.

Bael stares at her for a moment, tilts his head, then looks back at the boys and asks, "I know you haven't tried many new things. How about I introduce you to ooey—gooey pizza with every topping you can think of?"

Huxley speaks up first and screams, "YES, YES, YES!"

Peter says, "Their Hawaiian pizza is pretty good."

Omar chuckles and asks, "Hawaiian...like does it come with a hula dancer?"

Peter turns to Omar and says flatly, "You're such a moron."

"Better than more-off, I s'pose!"

Peter slaps his forehead leaving a soft pink handprint. "What does that even mean?"

"You don't get it? More *off*, not more *on*."

Bael quietly watches the exchange, then orders more pizza than even the entire foster home could eat, including the Portly Lady. He orders a pizza with cheese, one with pepperoni, another with sausage, still another with all meat, and more, and more, and more. He orders unlimited sodas, garlic knots, dessert pizzas, and boneless chicken tenders for Sully—cut into bite-sized pieces.

Huxley gasps, "This is going to cost more than the foster home would spend on us in—in—in a year! Maybe even two years!"

Bael says, "My children—as long as you're with *me*—you won't have to worry about *human* money."

"But—but I saw you give the Portly Lady some money,"

says Zack. "What was that for then?"

Appraising Zack with a watchful eye, he chose his next words carefully. "Zack, they need money because they are weak. I, however, am not weak. You'll learn that if you haven't already surmised as much with those watchful eyes of yours."

Huxley waits patiently for a break in the conversation, rolls up his sleeves, and announces that he'll be back.

Peter asks, "Where are you going?"

"I'm going to the kitchen to help them make the pizza."

Bael lets out a chuckle, "Huxley, they are going to cook for *us* tonight."

"O-okay, but should do the dishes after?"

"No, they will do the dishes, too."

Huxley's eyes brighten. It took four servers to carry out all the food and drinks to the table. There is little further talk as the foster kids scarf down the pizza, releasing various bodily noises with each progressive slice, like the sound of a barking seal.

Peter, on the other hand, doesn't touch a single slice of pizza. Not one garlic knot. Not even a sliver of the specialty pizza that Bael was sure to order, sans a hula dancer. Instead, he picks up the chicken bites and throws them to Sully one at a time. Each time the dog catches a delectable taste, gooey dog slobber from his mouth flies onto the table behind him. One glop even made it into a woman's Sprite with a soft plop just as she was picking it up to take a sip. Peter turns his head before the woman looks at him but breaks out into a fit of laughter at the loud sound of her straw sucking up the last droplets from the cup.

Bael whispers to Peter, "You're starting to feel it now, aren't you?"

"Yeah. It's weird. I'm not the least bit hungry and feel more energized than ever."

"Excellent."

Bael motions for the waitress. She approaches and says, "Sir, if there isn't anything else you need, I'll set the check right over here." She removes the check from her apron pocket and places it squarely on the table.

"Yes—yes, there is something else I need." Fixing his powerful gaze upon her, "You are not charging me for this. In fact, we're going to the arcade next. You'll go and fetch me all the quarters you have. Do you understand me?"

Her face transforms from a pretty soft pink glow to a morose, blank stare. She has a slight twitch to the left side of her face. Her shoulders drop, and her lips stiffen. Her nose makes a nasally sound as she absently replies, "Yes—sir. Arcade—quarters."

She turns on her heels and slowly drags each foot like they had fallen asleep as she stumbles to the cash register. She presses a button, and it makes a loud *ding*. The register drawer pops open, revealing its contents. Lifting the drawer holding the bills, she removes six rolls of quarters in the storage compartment below. Not even bothering to return the drawer and its overflowing bills, she returns to Bael and drops the quarters onto the table with a thud. The thin paper wrappers break open, releasing quarters onto the table like a slot machine at a casino.

"Arcade—quarters." Looking like a member of the Queen's Guard, she sharply turns on her heels and marches away.

Omar asks, "How do we split this up now? The papers are busted."

Zack answers, "That's easy. She brought four rolls of quarters over—each roll has 40 coins. There are four of us, assuming Bael doesn't want to play, we'll each get 40 quarters."

Huxley looks up and meekly replies, "Mr. Bael can have my quarters if he'd like."

Bael replies, "Huxley, you take the quarters for yourself. My fun will be watching you boys enjoy yourselves."

Peter squeals, "What are we waiting for? I love that place. Let's go, people!"

They theatrically throw their hands over their pizza-laden stomachs and uncomfortably moan as they make their way between the tables and leave the restaurant. They stagger across the street to the Barrel of Fun. The entrance is shaped like a huge brown barrel with flashing bright lights and music. A woman stands just outside the door donning a camouflage-colored ranger uniform with a wide-brimmed olive hat with a tall center dent.

Peter turns to Bael and says, "It looks like she's wearing a loaf of bread on her head!"

"Sir," says the loaf-wearing attendant, "I'm sorry. But dogs aren't allowed inside. You can tie him up on the bike rack."

Zack rounds on her and responds, "How about I tie you up instead!"

Sully jumps up and plants a great big sloppy kiss on Zack's face as if understanding him.

"Sir," looking straight at Bael, "perhaps you wish to tie that one up, too," she says as she wags her finger at Zack.

Omar lets out a wicked laugh and snickers, "I like her, but what's a loaf? Is it somethin' ya' push out?"

Zack indignantly responds to the woman, "The restaurant across the street let him in. Do you mean to tell me that some stupid arcade won't?"

Bael turns to the worker and makes eye contact with her. His eyes flash, and he starts walking without even looking back. "Come, Sully!"

Peter turns to Zack and says, "They have this really cool two-person racing game. Do you want to play it with me?"

"Yeah!" Zack runs after Peter to the back of the arcade. The game takes up the entire rear-left corner of the building. There are two shiny motorcycles, with each player getting his own ride. One is bright blue with yellow flames running down along the side. The other is a deep crimson red with a colorful fire-breathing dragon running down its full length. The exhaust pipe is fashioned like the base of the dragon's tail, coming to life as the game starts.

Peter pushes Zack aside and quickly runs to the red bike—each depositing four quarters on their respective sides of the machine. There are a variety of trails from which to choose. Zack's eyes light up as he looks at the description of each track. Before offering his input, Peter selects a medieval course, especially suited to his fire-breathing dragon motorcycle.

They ride their motorcycles with the agility of professional racers as they turn their bodies to the left and to the right—deftly avoiding collisions with obstacles in their paths, including each other. They each pull back with the full force of their body weight as they jump and skid over the rough terrain.

"Hey," yells Zack, "how did you get so good at this?"

"I've played this game hundreds of times!"

"So, you've been here before?"

"Oh, um, no. I've just played this game in other places."

Zack asks, "So what's the farm like?"

"It's a farm. If you've seen one, you've seen them all."

"I guess that's the problem. I haven't. Are there riding trails and things for us to do?"

Peter takes a second to respond. "Um, yeah, lots to do!"

"Is it far away?"

"No."

"Was that your first time at that pizza restaurant?"

"Enough with the questions already. Freshlings are so annoying!"

"What did you just call me?"

"Never mind."

Meanwhile, Omar's face lights up as he spots a game with a large machine gun. He pulls out four quarters and deposits them into the machine. It lights up and begins whirling and vibrating as Omar shoots at everything in his path—friends and enemies alike.

"Cool! So, this is what I've been missing!" His bellowing voice echoes off the walls as he screams, "DIE, DIE, DIE!"

Huxley slowly circles the arcade several times before stopping at a 3D dancing game. He slowly steps onto the game's dance floor. He awkwardly scrolls through song after song and eventually presses the button labeled "pick for me." He deposits two quarters into the machine, and the game directs him to build his avatar. He selects boy—small frame—light brown hair— brown eyes. His eyes bulge as the avatar flashes to life and invites him to dance.

The little circles on the dance floor light up, and he immediately jumps back. His avatar taunts him to return to the dance floor and instructs him to step on the circles as they light up. The music plays loudly, and the video screen shows his avatar dancing to the beat. He jumps back on the dance floor and follows along. Sully excitedly paces back and forth, then leaps onto the dance floor, too. He nips at Huxley's feet every time he jumps, causing Huxley to squeal with delight.

They spend a few hours at the arcade. Bael calls just once for them to leave. The three foster boys and Sully run to him at once. Peter, however, needs a few *pointed* commands to leave the arcade.

Once Peter reluctantly returns to Bael, he whines, "I'm tired of walking. Can we do the..."

Bael booms, "SHUSH."

Peter's eyes bulge like they are a popcorn kernel getting ready to pop.

"We have to walk with the freshlings."

"Forever? They're worse than dogs!"

"Just until they have finished serving their purpose." Bael sighs, "Okay—okay. There's a hotel about a mile up the road. We'll stop there for the night."

"Is someone going to say something about you having four boys and a dog? Like that waitress did?"

"Have you noticed that there are others who seek my approval?"

"What do you mean?"

"They have been following us. Every time I draw energy from the freshlings, they can feel it and come sniffing around like a dog searching for a bone."

"Was one of them at the pizza restaurant?"

"Yes."

Peter drags his feet along the tattered old sidewalk and nearly trips over a particularly tall group of weeds that had forced their way through the cracks. Sully examines the weeds, does a few quick circles, and relieves himself. Omar walks up behind the dog, plucks a reed, puts it into his mouth, and feverishly chews on it as they walk.

They continue until they approach a sign advertising "The Teepee Motel." The foyer looks like a teepee with painted Native American script in a dazzling array of colors. Men are wearing long, feathered headdresses with painted faces riding atop beautifully majestic horses. An array of stunningly painted red and gold inverted triangles litter the base of the wall. The archway leading inside looks just like the curved entrance of a real teepee. There are thirteen poles adorned with white lights spread out equally at the floor and reaching towards each other and tied off on top. There is even a fireplace in the center of the room, just like an authentic teepee.

The beautiful mirrors adorning either side of the lobby make the sparkling lights even more alluring—casting their bright multi-colored lights in every direction. There is a table set up with several glass jars reading "Buffalo Beef Jerky" please help yourself. Two large self-circulating glass drink dispensers read "Native American Sassy Frassy Tea—please fill a glass with ice cubes and enjoy." The boys enter first and let out feelings of awe. The sparkling dog tag dangling from Sully's collar begins to pulsate and glow like sunlight reflected through a prism. Bael meanders into the hotel last. The smile on his face at once replaced with a look of pained fear.

"NO!" Bael's posture changes in one quick breath.

He's no longer standing upright and beautiful but hunched over, ragged, and with a flood of gray hair replacing his blond locks.

"We're—NOT—staying!"

Bael turns around and quickly heads for the door. Thick beads of sweat drip down from his brow. Sully beats him to the door and turns on him. Baring his sharp canine teeth and growling with the viciousness of a mother bear protecting her cubs. The hair from his shoulder blades to his tailbone stands up at full attention. His collar comes to life with captivating colors pouring from it like a disco ball. The dog does not budge when Bael yells at him to move. His legs are sturdy and wide, giving a keen resemblance to those of a bulldog.

Peter throws the dog aside and grabs Bael's arm, draping it over his shoulders. He supports most of Bael's body weight as they scamper out the door like white-tailed rabbits in the thralls of an approaching falcon. Omar—followed next by Huxley—plunge their hands into the jar and fish out a large handful of jerky. Omar shoves his catch into his mouth all at one time. Huxley chews on one piece and places the rest in his pocket. The two then turn on their heels and follow Bael and Peter.

The hotel clerk donning Native American attire looks at Zack with a look of concern stretched across her face. "Young man, is everything okay?"

"Um, I'm not quite sure. This place is amazing!"

"Then why did your friends leave?"

"That's a really good question." Shrugging his shoulders, he says, "I wish I knew."

They bitterly trudge down the road for a few more miles. Just as they are about to reach the outskirts of town, a police cruiser slows down as he spies the motley crew looking peculiarly out of place. Zack and Sully trail at the back end of their group.

Rolling down his window, the police officer asks Zack, "Hey son, where are you heading?"

Zack answers, "I'm—uh—well..."

He stops blubbering because a black-cloaked figure is barreling right down the sidewalk and directly towards him on a bicycle. With barely a moment to spare, Zack pulls Sully back and they fall to the ground as the man zips right cycles right past him with the enthuasism of someone ready to cross the finish line. The cloaked figure pulls one of his feet from the bike and strikes the police cruiser, causing the car's exterior to fold like a balled up piece of aluminum foil.

Peter's mouth drops open and he turns to Bael. "Was that a—a—a dark elf?"

"Yes."

"But how? Why?"

"I am close to having enough power to be *the one.*"

"The one?"

"The ruler of the dark elves."

"What do you have to do to be *the one?*"

"I need that amulet back that you found. The one that was stolen from me thirteen years ago."

The two continue walking in silence. They pass glorified shacks used as homes. Most don't have any windows, but the few that do have bars on them. Sully inches closer and closer to Zack and eventually hits the side of his leg as they pass nefarious-looking people sitting outside. An old man stares intently at Sully and jumps up like he's just won a game of bingo, abandoning the walking stick sitting beside him. Stretching out his bony fingers, he reaches for the dog's collar. Sully lets out a ferocious bark and makes contact with several of his crooked fingers. The old man pulls his hand back, flips it over, and ferociously swings at the dog's head. But before making contact, Zack catches his hand with his own and squeezes hard, draining all remaining color from his pale skin. The man falls to his knees and lets out a deafening cry. Crows perched upon the overhead powerlines mimic the sound of the man's scream. Zack throws the man's hand back down with such a vengeance that it bounces off the sidewalk.

Through gritted teeth, Zack slowly says, "Now—try—that—again—and—watch—what I'll—do—to—you!"

"You stupid child! You will see!"

"See what, old man?"

"The eyes. They watch everything. You can't escape them. They're everywhere. Make a little oath, did you?"

"Well—I..."

"That dog of yours..."

"What about him?"

"He's no ordinary dog."

The man turns his head and spits on Zack's tattered old sneaker. Zack's face contorts in disgust. He reflexively lifts his foot to examine the viscous substance, then smartly wipes it onto the side of the man's wrinkled, bare leg. Sully watches with his big brown eyes and lets out a forceful sneeze in the man's direction, then he and Zack set off after the rest of the group.

Peter continues to support Bael's bodyweight as they hobble along, not making much progress.

"Yo, Petey," bellows Omar. "Yous want me to take over?"

"First, my name is Peter, not Petey. You'd better remember that. Second, I don't want you anywhere near him."

Huxley intently watches the exchange with his eyes darting back and forth like a tennis match. Omar puffs his chest up.

"Petey, you gonna do somethin' 'bout it?"

"Just who do you think you are, freshling?"

"Duh—my name's Omar." He lifts his big fist and drops it just as fast when Bael's blue eyes shift and focus upon him.

They walk a few steps further in silence as they approach another hotel a few doors down from the shacks. It's a dump and makes the group home look like a five-star hotel. Bael whispers something to Peter, who, in turn, instructs the boys to wait outside. Omar and Huxley hunker down and discuss video games. Sully finds a nice place to leave his *mark*, kicks up the dirt and grass up around him, and buries his business. Zack opens his mouth wide and laughs. A chunk of grass and dirt hits him squarely on the back of his throat, causing him to swallow reflexively. He tries to loosen the dirt and grass like a cat releasing a furball.

Several minutes pass. Peter stomps his feet and pushes on the hotel door to leave, but as he pushes, one of the hinges snaps off. He looks back at the hotel clerk, who shrugs and says, "That door's been falling off its hinges for ages now. One good whack and I'll get it fixed as good as new; don't you worry."

Peter responds sarcastically, "I'll try my best."

Taking a few steps back out into the parking lot, Peter stumbles as he fit falls into a pothole. He rolls his eyes and motions for Bael to walk with him, but now keeping his eyes on the obstacle course in front of him. Their voices are soft, but their body posture reveals a heated dispute between the two. Peter dramatically throws his hands up in the air and mouths the word, "No."

Bael points his long finger at Peter's beautiful blue eyes. Peter lets out a sigh, shakes his head up and down, then hangs his head and kicks a pebble on the ground.

Bael announces to the group, "We're staying here tonight. Follow me."

They all enter through the broken door and leave it wagging back and forth on its hinges. This hotel doesn't have mirrors, a pool, a hot tub, or an arcade. Instead, it has the gaudiest pink and green wallpaper peeling from the walls. It's almost as though the wallpaper doesn't even want to be there. There's a sign announcing, "RESTROOM IS FOR PAYIN' FOLKS ONLY/TOILET PAPER IS 1¢ PER SQUARE-SOAP IS 5¢ PER SQUIRT—SEE CLERK."

The air is choked by the pungent smell of cigarette smoke. Sully begins a fit of violent sneezing that gets so bad he starts passing gas and sneezing at the same time. Huxley is downwind from the dog and cries out when he gets a full blast of his gas.

The carpeting was once a creamy texture of pinks, yellows, and greens swirling into beautiful designs. Now is a receptacle for cigarette smoke, ground-in dirt, and an assortment of stains. Zack's eyes bulge as he looks at the carpet and back at Sully who is now lifting his paw to his mouth.

Darting towards the dog, Zack strains, but manages to pick up the sneezing and gassy dog and cradle him in his arms. Sully looks up at him and plants a wet kiss spanning from his chin to his forehead.

Bael gives Peter a smart push towards the desk clerk, who dons a handwritten name tag that reads "Billy Joe." His poorly cut brown hair mirrors Huxley's hair. His green eyes speak to a simple life with very few experiences outside of the run-down hotel. Not to mention the crooked smile he proffers with coffee-stained teeth and a bulbous nose dotted with acne in various states of healing.

Bael leans against the putrid wall with one leg bent and resting against the wall. He patiently watches and waits like a praying mantis waiting for its kill. Watches and waits. Watches and waits. Omar picks up a decade-old pamphlet and studies it until his eyes cross. He repeatedly flips it over, shakes his head, then throws it to the floor. He eyeballs Huxley and begins to tease him. Zack pulls up his hood, falls back into a dark corner, and just quietly watches the scene unfolding before him as he continues to cradle the floppy dog who has lazily collapsed in his arms.

After a considerable length of time, Peter's voice turns into a maniacal yell. Bael sighs and approaches the counter, gently pushing Peter aside. Billy Joe's gaze quickly goes blank. His white skin turns a rosy pink, now complementing the color of his acne. He slowly nods his head up and down in response to Bael's voice and hands him a key. The two turn around and walk away from the yellow-stained counter. Peter's eyes begin to dull and quickly change shade—still blue, only less so.

Bael turns around and walks towards Zack. "Put the dog down and find the room."

Zack puts down the lazy dog just in time as Bael flings the key at his face. They walk down an outdoor hallway and pass by an assortment of questionable looking characters. With no other option, they walk past a man standing outside donning only his boxer shorts and a blue and red polka-dotted tie. He is deep in the thralls of a lively conversation—with only himself.

"What should we have for supper tonight?" he asks.

He turns to the other side, throws up his arms, and replies to himself, "It's your turn to pick!"

Turning to the other side, he cries back to himself, "No, I picked yesterday."

Turning again and this time screaming, "No, I picked yesterday."

Peter laughs and says, "Be careful. You might give yourself whiplash!"

The boxer bandit looks up at Peter. He takes hold of his gluttonous stomach and rounds on Peter. With a flash, Bael is right behind the man. He reaches out and touches the man's bare shoulder causing him to cry out and fall to the ground—his stomach jiggling in waves like jello. Beyond him, a couple is sitting on bright pink beach chairs. Their feet are soaking in an ankle-deep inflatable pool filled with brown water. They are each wearing a round life preserver around their waists.

A little further down, there's a group of five electrical workers using the boom from their company's line truck to carry each other from the ground to the second story landing. Both the one operating the controls and the dummy in the bucket are blindfolded. It looks like a foolhardy attempt at pin the tail on the moron. One man misses the second-story railing, and Huxley rushes to his aid. He bravely throws his tiny arms over the bar and screams for the man to take hold. The blindfolded man waves his arms through the air as he tries to make contact in the area of the boy's voice. He pulls Huxley forward so hard that his head bounces off the iron railing, leaving an imprint on the boy's sweaty forehead. The boy still doesn't let go. After a moment or two of intense tugging, the man climbs over the railing and flops onto the second-story walkway.

Zack announces, "Well, here we are. The paradise known as Room 213."

They make their way into the room. A pungent smell immediately assaults them. It wreaks of body odor and urine. The sunlight shines brightly through the window and reveals a cloud of dust floating through the air.

Zack says, "You know, this dust contains human skin cells."

Omar exclaims, "That don' even make sense! Skin don' have no cells. Just people! Why would skin be calling on cell phones?"

Zack's face contorts, he shakes his head, and mumbles, "Moron!"

"Thanks! Like I says, good to me more-on than more-off!"

"Get out of the way," Peter barks as he roughly pushes past Zack and Omar and collapses on the very first bed, succumbing to complete exhaustion even before the last person has entered the room.

The other boys engage in a fierce bed-to-bed jumping competition. Peter doesn't stir an inch as they jump near his head, looking much more like a bear during hibernation than a tired teen.

Sully watches eagerly from the floor and begins whining and pacing back and forth. He seems to think twice, then excitedly propels his entire body onto one of the beds and joins in the competition. With aerodynamics in his favor, along with the dog's lean and muscular body, he crushes them all. The three boys eventually jump to the vacant bed one last time and pile up in a mound on top of Huxley. The stack-o-boys on top of him fall asleep and don't hear his begging and pleading to move. Not that it would have mattered if they did. His little arms and legs manage to slowly inch out from the pileup before he collapses, too, into a deep sleep.

Morning arrives, and Bael shakes them wildly like upturned saltshakers. Huxley cries out and jumps up. He throws his tiny hands against his heart that's now beating like an out of control war drum. Zack and Omar take a little more prodding, but the mention of breakfast manages to stir them. Bael bends down and whispers something in Peter's ear and gently lifts him to a sitting position. Sully sticks out his warm, wet tongue and licks Peter's face from his chin—passing over his lips—and landing on the outside of his eyelids.

The dog excitedly tries to free the eye boogers from both eyes when Peter announces, "I'm awake, I'm awake!"

They leave the hotel room and set out walking towards the hotel restaurant. A yellowed sign advertises "Breakfast Any Way You'd Like It." The picture shows greasy hash browns that can slide right down your throat and still have enough grease to come back up, thick slabs of bacon, and eggs served any way you want, but they must be scrambled.

As they wait for their slop to be served, Zack asks, "Hey, Peter, have your eyes always been that sparkling shade of blue?"

"Duh—yeah."

"I guess I just never noticed. So, tell me about school. Do you have a lot of friends?"

"It's cool. I have homework and stuff. But I guess it's what you have to do if you want to be somebody. Right?"

Omar blurts out, "I ain't doing no homework!"

Zack ignores him and says, "Yeah, I guess so. Are you on any teams?"

"Loads! I'm on the football and baseball teams."

"Sweet! That's cool. Both sports have different seasons, so I'm sure you don't get bored."

"Ugh—yeah. Food's here. Time to eat."

"Yeah, if that's what you'd call it!" Zack says as he raises the side of his lip in absolute disgust. He picks up the plate and tilts it slightly, watching the food slide to the side and leaving a trail of grease behind. "I've seen snails leave less goo behind them than this stuff."

Zack quietly picks up his plate and puts it on the floor with a soft clink. Sully doesn't seem to have a problem eating it—or perhaps it's because the dog eats so fast his brain doesn't have time to register its greasy taste. Then again, dogs also lick their butts.

They leave the restaurant and begin walking down a lonely stretch of highway. The once lush and vibrant landscape mirrors the look on Zack's face: depressed and dead on the inside. He walks without talking.

Bael looks at him. "You're quiet today. Is everything okay?"

"Yeah—yeah. I'm just not much of a talker."

"I understand. Maybe you can rub off on Peter."

Chuckling, "Yeah, I don't think that's going to happen. Hey, if you don't mind me saying, you and Peter look an awful lot alike. Your eyes—they're identical."

"Indeed."

"So why is that? Are you two distant relatives or something? And that cloaked figure who hit the police car—his eyes were blue, too. And I swear I can see blue eyes staring out at us as we walk."

"Zack, you ask too many questions. You need to stop for your own safety."

"Safety?"

Bael looks intently at Zack with his pulsating ice blue eyes. Zack feels a sharp pain behind his eyes and at once begins to blink rapidly. Bael's eyes change from pulsating blue to a look of bewilderment.

Zack throws his hands to his forehead. "Are you doing something to me right now? I feel—weird."

"Interesting. But there you go again with the questions. That's going to get you into trouble. Trouble you aren't going to be able to get yourself out of."

Chapter 16

Bael and Peter talk in hushed voices as Omar, Huxley, and Zack trail behind them. Sully has a case of the doggy *zoomies* and is running in exaggerated circles like something is chasing him—hampered only by alternating tail nub chases.

Zack finally breaks the silence. "Don't you two think it's a bit weird they keep talking to each other and not to us?"

"Well, the foster care staff didn't talk to us either," answers Huxley.

Omar says, "Dunno know. Don' care."

"Have you noticed they get quiet every time we get closer to them?" asks Zack.

"No," reply Omar and Huxley in unison.

Zack orders, "Huxley, go walk closer to them. Let's see if they stop talking."

"Uh-okay," agrees Huxley.

Zack and Omar fix their gazes on Huxley as he gets closer to Bael and Peter. Just as Zack had predicted, their talking stops. They both look at Huxley, then Bael eerily turns back and makes eye contact with Zack—but not Omar. An entire conversation happens in that brief moment that their eyes meet.

"Peter, you know what to do," says Bael.

Peter turns and looks directly at Huxley. His eyes pulsate and shine an intense, brilliant blue. "You need to go back there with Zack and Omar. Do you understand me?"

Huxley's face flushes, and his eyes go blank and emotionless. His small frame becomes rigid like rigormortous had set in, and he absently replies in a monotone voice. "Yes—yes— I—understand." He turns and walks back to them.

Zack waits a few minutes until there is some space separating them and asks, "Hey, what did they say to you?"

He replies, "Umm—I—umm—I—I—don't—know."

"Do you two *still* think it's safe to be with them?" asks Zack.

Omar answers first, "Dude, we get whatever we want and don' have to pay for nothin'."

Huxley says, "Well, I'm not hungry anymore. I was always hungry at the foster home. I had to—had to—well, I was hungry."

"So, you two are happy with them?"

"Yeah," grunts Omar.

"Sure," squeaks Huxley.

"But don't you think that too much of what they said just doesn't make sense?" Zack asks.

Omar asks, "Um, what do you mean? We don' need no *cents* with them. Bael don' use no money," boasts Omar.

"I thought you was the smart one. The one who can read and all."

Zack hides a laugh. "Okay, let me break it down for you. For starters, how can Peter be both on the football AND the soccer teams when he just started school a week ago?"

"Maybe—maybe he was on—on those teams at his old school," suggests Huxley.

"Okay, that would make sense. Um...I mean, that sounds like it could be right, but he also said that Bael makes him do his homework and stuff. IF they just met a week ago and spent most of that time walking to the foster home, how would he have any homework? He hasn't even had time to go to school yet. Not even for a single day by my count. And what grown man walks this much? Why doesn't he have a car? If he owns a farm, you'd think he could afford a car."

"Uh, I dunno," says Omar.

"He also said that he's never been to that pizza restaurant and arcade before."

Omar says, "So, that don' mean nothin'."

"Well, that's a pretty stupid thing to lie about. So why'd he do it?"

Omar shrugs, and Huxley throws his hands out.

"And why did Bael flip his lid when he walked into the fancy hotel with the mirrors? And those freaky eyes. Peter has them, too. Did you notice?"

Omar and Huxley don't respond.

"And I think Peter is somehow getting stronger. It's like their minds are connected, and they don't even have to talk. Like the time when Peter wasn't paying attention and almost walked off the cement embankment and right into the river. Do you remember that? Bael didn't yell to him like anyone else would have, but somehow signaled the danger to Peter. Peter looked up just in time."

Still no response.

Zack asks, "Do you two want to leave with me? We can come up with a plan to get away from them."

"And do what?" cries Huxley.

"If we stick around with these two, who knows what will happen to us. You see how he can play those mind tricks on people. I swear he tried it on me already. I think they just did the same thing to you, Huxley."

"I don't want to go back to the group home," Huxley says with tears forming in his eyes. "I had to eat from—from..."

"Not me!" says Omar.

"Well, you two had better not get in my way, then," Zack says defiantly.

Omar puffs up, pounds one fist into the other, "Or—what?"

"Just don't stop me is all I'm saying."

Just then Bael and Peter stop without warning. Omar and Huxley follow suit. Zack is still staring off—lost in thought and walks right into Omar. He turns on Zack, cocks his fist back, and sends a punch straight towards Zack's face. But when his fist is about to make contact with Zack's nose, something pulls him back. Zack's widened eyes scan in every direction to see why Omar's fist didn't make contact with his face. The only thing that's remotely close to him is Peter who is intently watching the two of them.

Zack gasps, "Peter—what—just—happened?"

Peter stares at him—his blue eyes blazing like a solar

flare.

"Did *you* stop him?"

"Maybe."

"But you're so far away. He's so strong."

Peter answers, "Your point?"

"Oh, well, um. Nothing."

They continue walking several blocks, and the street widens and now accommodates six lanes of traffic. The noise of passing cars, sirens, and blasting horns permeate the rushing river water's once serene sound. On the left is a variety of restaurants. Zack tilts his head as he notices, "The Roadkill Café."

He looks at Sully and says, "Buddy, you'd better watch out. If you walk out into the road and get hit, they'll serve you up for dinner on a bun with a choice of finger-licking barbecue sauce!"

On the right, there is a sign along a row of lush trees with twinkling white lights that reads "The Sharmike Resort."

Peter's eyes sparkle, and he turns to Bael. "I've always wanted to stay here." He then turns to the boys and says, "Stay here. Do you understand me?"

Omar's face has the same blank stare as always, but Huxley's sweet and innocent expression changes. His face reddens, his body stiffens like his clothes are two sizes too small, and his eyes—the window to his sweet soul—just stare right past Peter. The two do as they are told and do not move. Zack just looks at them all—saying nothing. Buying his time. His facial expression and body posture remain unchanged. Peter and Bael look at each other—then back at Zack. Peter shrugs and walks towards the hotel lobby.

In a few minutes, Peter returns with the keys and a huge smile on his face. He looks at Bael, puffs his chest, and announces, "Dinner will be served in one hour." Bael shoots him an approving glance. "We'd better hurry up because the walk through the lobby is...quite interesting!"

The hotel lobby looks like an extravagant indoor greenhouse. Several stoned paths swirl around a variety of ecosystems. The first sign they approach reads *La Tropicale*. There's a variety of flora and fauna on this path reminiscent of its name. There's a procession of palm trees wrapped with beautiful white lights and colorful parrots perched upon them that seem to be in the middle of a lively conversation. Omar stops to look at the coconuts growing on the palm trees.

Omar orders, "Zack, read that sign."

"Okay. It's about coconuts. It says that coconuts were used as grenades by the Japanese during World War II. They hurled them at their enemies. Hey, did you know that coconuts kill about 150 people every year—that's 15 times more than are chomped to death by sharks.

Omar screams, "Wow. Palm trees are my new favorite plant!"

Peter scoffs, "You idiot! They're trees, not plants!"

Zack interrupts and says, "Actually, trees are just a type of plant that's learned how to steal the most sun."

Omar shoots Peter a dirty look. "Yeah, everyone knows that."

Huxley stops at the banana tree and studies the growing bananas. He turns to Omar and says, "It says that the main part of the tree is called the throat. The trees only grow one bunch of bananas per year or about 200 bananas. The rows—"

Omar pushes past him. "Bor—ing!"

Peter stops at the spider exhibit. There are hundreds of tangle web spiders crawling around. He reads that the spiders have become more aggressive over time as the strong spiders are more likely to survive in their unforgiving, harsh tropical climate with its devastating storms. He continues to read that these spiders are known to become even more aggressive than they already are if they become overly hot.

Peter flashes his eyes. The inside of the exhibit starts to fill with smoke. The reddish-brown arachnid in front of him looks like a cousin to a black widow. The spider doesn't catch on fire, but it does start to move in a fit of fury. It quickly maneuvers over its web, finds a smaller spider, swiftly attacks it, and then ravenously consumes it. Zack watches Peter as a devilish smile consumes his face.

The end of the path forks with two more paths: *Into the Wild* on the left and *Paradise Path* on the right. They enter *Into the Wild* next. It's like a rainforest complete with a deep jungle, an overhead green canopy, and blue morpho butterflies flitting about. An enamored pair of scarlet macaws proudly display their fanciful blue, yellow, and red plumage. The signage reads that they were born in captivity at the hotel about ten years ago and will remain bonded for their entire lives, living for nearly fifty years.

Peter yells out, "Hey, Bael. Isn't that how old you are?"

He ignores Peter's jibe and walks towards the poison dart frog enclosure filled with brightly colored frogs. The sign reads, "POISON—TOXIC VENOM, DO NOT TOUCH!" Bael reaches his hands in and proceeds to pick one up and put it in his pocket.

Peter cries out, "Bael, are you crazy! Those are poisonous! I'm not carrying you if you get sick!"

Omar leans to Zack and says, "I guess I'm not the only one who can't read."

Bael whispers to Peter, "The poison from these frogs can be put inside the tips of darts. Just one of these is enough to kill ten fully grown men."

Peter smiles and asks, "Can I have one, too?"

"Peter, everything I have is yours."

"No kidding! Well, see...I want..."

"Do I have to remind you what I have in my pocket this *very moment?*"

Peter does a little uncomfortable chuckle and then falls back several steps behind Bael.

Their last trek is through the *Paradise Path.* It has a beautiful array of ponds and waterfalls. Lightning storms let out sharp sounds every hour with holographic moving images of overhead storm clouds. Rain falls from the ceiling and replenishes the water circulated in other areas of the exhibits. The sound of the falling water is almost as mesmerizing as Bael. Their excitement turns to panic as Sully jumps into one of the beautifully landscaped ponds and catches a giant orange and white koi fish. It writhes and squirms in his mouth.

Zack gulps loudly. "Come on, boy. I have a nice little snack for you right here," as he holds out his cupped hand. He now has Sully's attention. "That's right. You don't want that yucky fish. Just drop it. That's right. Spit him out!"

He finally lures the dog out of the water. The dog opens his mouth, and the fish falls to the floor with a smack! Zack scoops it up and gently tosses it back into the pond. Sully sniffs Zack's hand and huffs. Then violently shakes the water off him and onto Zack.

"Swell. Eau de wet dog! Now I need a shower."

They leave the exhibits and find their suite, which is an exhibit all its own. Each of the boys has his own bed encased in a tent resembling a string of tiny sailboats. Each tent is complete with more pillows than all the hotels they have visited—combined. There is a giant pirate ship leading to the bathroom. You must climb the steps to enter the restroom. If someone uses the bathroom but fails to wash his hands, the stairs close, and that person has to walk the plank to exit. Omar was the first to discover that fun fact.

Breathing heavy—it's now—or never. Zack takes a deep breath and climbs the steps leading to the bathroom. The sign on the wood-paneled door reads, "Welcome to the head, matey!" He opens the door to see a toilet and a shower in the same room. The water from the shower drains directly into a drainage hole in the center of the room. The shower has a really long hose that's several feet longer than necessary.

"I bet you can go to the bathroom AND take a shower at the same time."

He locks the door with a loud CLICK. He pulls out the butter knife he had pocketed from the diner earlier that day. He carefully starts to unscrew the wall-mounted, round mirror shaped like a porthole. A screw slips out of his sweaty hands and CLANKS onto the faux wooden floor made of ceramic tile. Figures!

"ZACK— what's going on in there?" yells Bael.

"Ugh— *nothing,*" he replies, using too high of a pitch in his voice. Lowering it, "I'm—just—just —just getting ready to take a shower. All that walking made me—ugh—

sweaty!"

He turns on the shower and exhaust fan.

"Stupid! Why didn't I do that first?"

He quietly removes the last screw from the wall mount. Sweat is dripping down his forehead and pooling on the floor.

Taking a deep breath, he grasps the doorknob and slowly opens it, hitting Sully smartly in the head with the door. Startled, Sully lets out a yelp and jumps from the door. Omar and Huxley hear the commotion, pop their heads out of their tents, and look up towards Zack. He takes a startled breath and shuts the door with a start.

"Stupid! Stupid! Stupid!"

He breathes again as his whole chest puffs up—and falls back down—puffs up—and falls back down. Suddenly...BANG! He throws open the bathroom door, and it bounces off the wall and ricochets back on him. He pushes it out of the way, leaves the bathroom, and quickly scampers down the steps with the speed and agility of a mouse. Bael and Peter gasp when they see Zack appear with the mirror grasped tightly in his hands.

"I KNOW WHAT YOU ARE!"

Zack holds the mirror with both arms and angles it downward—forcing Bael to kneel before him. The mirror surges with a fierce electrical current. Zack's face furrows as he wraps his hands further up on the frame of the mirror. Bael's face becomes distorted. It elongates—stretches—pulls towards the mirror. His perfect appearance no longer perfect. His unnaturally long ears stretch even longer.

Weakly, Bael begs with a soft whisper to his voice, "Peter—you—must—stop—him."

Peter's mouth drops open, and his bulging eyes just blankly stare at the scene unfolding before him.

"Peter—you—must—stop—him! I'm—your—*real*—father! We—were—separated—when—you—were—just—a—baby! Please—please—son!"

Peter's already wide-open eyes somehow open even further. He asks, "You—you are?" He then looks around frantically and grabs the only thing he can find that isn't screwed down—the TV remote control. He chucks it at Zack with all his might. THUMP! It cracks him square in the center of his forehead. Blood starts to trickle down into his eyes. He holds on to the mirror with one hand and uses the other to wipe the blood away, switches the side holding the mirror, then continues to wipe more blood from his eyes. His slippery hands drop the mirror. As if in slow motion, it falls from his hands and hits the floor—smashing to smithereens.

Bael's face is no longer distorted and seems to snap back into place—no longer under the control of the mirror—but he's not getting up either. Zack's "deer in headlights" look wipes away, and he bends down and grabs a piece of the broken mirror. He grips it so hard his hand starts to bleed and falls into perfectly round droplets on the floor. He shakes his head in disbelief, turns on his heels, and dashes out of the hotel room.

"H—E—L—P!"

Bael commands Omar and Huxley, "GET HIM, YOU FOOLS!"

To Zack's dismay, Omar and Huxley do exactly as commanded. They quickly tear off in hot pursuit of him. Sully runs out of the hotel room and follows all three of them. He nips at the back of Omar's and Huxley's pants, causing them to fall hard to the floor. Huxley was the first to fall, and Omar lands right on top of him, stealing his breath away.

One by one, the other hotel room doors begin to open. The first door to open was of a plump man donning shaving cream on half of his face. "Hey!" but that's as far as he gets as he spits out the shaving cream that spilled into his mouth, causing him to gag and violently spit onto the floor.

The second door reveals a woman who is holding a screaming baby in her arms. "Quiet down out there! You woke up my baby!"

The third door opens, and there's a man in a full clown costume complete with face paint and a balloon animal in mid-creation. Red paint outlines his broad smile, displaced by downturned eyes that create a menacing appearance. Omar and Huxley don't seem to miss a beat as they quickly get back up. The clown looks to the right and sees Zack, followed by Sully, running in fear and screaming for help.

The clown looks to the left and notices Omar and Huxley chasing after the boy and dog. He quickly sticks out his foot, and Omar falls hard to the tile floor like a chopped tree. On his way down, he reaches out and grabs Huxley for support, but only succeeds in dragging him down, too. The clown walks up to them with his creepy smile and pulls out a baby boy toy. A swift pull on the toy's diaper causes it to pee on the two of them.

"Hey!" screams Omar, and some of the liquid goes into his mouth. He leaves a web of broken tile on the floor as he rolls over with his giant fists cocked and ready to fight. The clown quickly squeezes a little red horn and does a bow. He then backs into his hotel room and slams the door.

They get back up, and their feet slip on the watery substance. Huxley is too slow to catch Zack—but Omar is stronger and faster than both boys. He's right on Zack's tail, just like a defensive back in football. Zack takes off through the *Paradise Path* and ducks as the pair of macaws screech out, *"Errrot...he's gonna catch you! Errrot...he's gonna catch you! Errot...walk the plank. Errot...walk the plank!"*

Zack's feet slip, and he smashes right into the spider enclosure, causing it to shatter into hundreds of little pieces. Thousands of angry spiders spill out and are on the loose and thirsty for blood revenge. He and Sully make it out before any crawl on them, but Omar and Huxley aren't so lucky. He can hear their screams as spiders pierce their skin with their vicious fangs, buying Zack and Sully a slight lead as they round the path leading into *La Tropicale*.

An alarm rings out alerting the hotel staff to the broken enclosure. As Zack and Sully are within sight of the front door, the hotel staff run in the opposite direction to catch the spiders. Zack reaches out for the front door like a football player trying to score when Omar grabs him by the scruff of the neck. He throws Zack to the floor with such force that he bounces hard as his body hits the unforgiving cement floor. Zack struggles, but he can't break free from Omar's grasp.

Zack pleads, "Please! We need to get out of here! I'll do whatever you want! Please!"

Squeezing Zack's throat and nearly cutting off his air, "So you can control minds now, can you?"

"No—but..."

Squeezing even harder, "Not—a—chance—then!"

Zack closes his eyes. *"I'm on my way, Mom and Dad."*

He winces—but then—Sully bites Omar right on the butt, pulling him off by the back of his pants. Sully bounces up and down and continues to shred the pants and his meaty flesh. The sound of ripping pants and the wetness from Sully's mouth permeates the room. Zack throws his hands to the floor and gasps in a deep pull of air.

Sully quickly spits out the clothing and flesh like they're a putrid-tasting poison. The dog theatrically crosses the threshold into the lobby, throws himself to the carpet, and tries to wipe the blood from his face. He plants his face on the floor with his rear up in the air and violently transfers the blood from his face to the elegant floral-patterned carpet.

Suddenly, Zack's body begins to thin like a Stretch Armstrong toy. His face, arms, and legs painfully stretch in every direction like he's in the thralls of a medieval torture device. Bael and Peter have arrived. Even over Zack's screams, the buzzing sound of an invisible forcefield permeates the room. Zack stretches his hands out, trying to grasp at anything. His fingers pull against the floor—his nails folding back from their nail beds like peeling bananas. A mere arm's length from Bael and Peter—and Sully's collar begins to glow a weird sort of rainbow color in every direction.

Zack can see the once invisible force now showing a deep crimson color triangulated between Bael, Peter, and Sully—like the evil cousin of the Northern Lights. The dog puffs out his chest, bows out his legs, and stands his ground. He leans forward with his teeth bared and lets out a low, fierce growl. Bael and Peter lock hands, and their dazzling blue eyes come out to play. The dog is no match for the two of them. The crimson lasso wraps around Sully's four legs, and he falls to the ground—writhing in pain.

Zack pleads, "Stop! Stop! Punish me instead!"

Bael's mouth turns upward and he says, "As you wish."

Bael savors the joy of slowly tracing the outline of Zack's body with his eyes. Zack lies helplessly splayed out on the ground. The floor slowly begins to smoke, and then fire engulfs him like a circus performer's ring of fire. Sully's big eyes watch Zack as he lets out a long cry. The dog collar begins to glow brighter and brighter—like it has a mind of its own. There's a whoosh sound, and the collar sucks in the ring of fire and extinguishes it like a candle snuffer. The jeweled collar glows with fire within it, then grays with clouds of spreading smoke.

The crimson lasso unties and floats in the air like the brief cloud left behind from a sparkler. Sully looks at Peter and blinks twice. The lasso wraps around Peter's feet, throwing him to the ground. Zack jumps up, grabs Sully, and the two run full throttle out the door and flee into the surrounding woods.

Peter screams, "THEY'RE GETTING AWAY!"

Bael just raises his eyes and says, "They won't get far."

Chapter 17

Bael, Peter, Omar, and Huxley wind through the exhibits and return to the stillness of the hotel room and gather what few personal belongings they each have. Not having anything, Huxley sits and watches as Omar looks over his shoulder, darts his eyes at the location of Bael and Peter, and scampers up the ladder and into the bathroom.

"Let's go, Omar," orders Bael. "We're leaving NOW."

While in the bathroom, Omar quickly relieves himself and opens the door. Forgetting to wash his hands, he walks the plank one last time.

Bael angrily demands, "Quit playing around, Omar!"

Peter says, "No, I think he's just that dumb. He didn't learn his lesson the last time this happened. I told you."

Huxley quickly turns his head to avoid receiving Peter's barrage of insults. Omar shoots a dirty look at Peter but says nothing. They leave the room, and the door closes with a thud. Several hotel guests are still gathered in a small group and are in a deep conversations when they look up and see Bael.

The onlookers cast unapproving stares at Bael and the boys.

The clown gets high up on his toes, blasts his little horn, and says, "The police are coming to take you to the big house, and I'm not talking about the big top!"

Bael flashes his eyes at the clown's red nose and sets in on fire. The clown frantically runs in small circles, sounding his ridiculous horn. The woman standing beside him yanks on the daisy clipped to his lapel. She pulls on the retractable string, points it at his nose, pushes the button several times, and the flower spits out water and extinguishes his nose.

The foursome quietly make their way through the labyrinth of paths. They leave the lobby and head towards the thick bracken behind the hotel in Zack and Sully's general direction. The silence is deafening. It's like the world just stopped existing beyond them. There's not a sound to be heard. The soft-plumaged thrushes are not suppling their usual bounty of inspiration for poets and musicians. The ever-popular songs of the wrens do not sound. The flaming sounds coming from the orioles have been extinguished. The melody of sparrows and finches with their sophisticated warbling are at bay. Flowers do not deposit their pollen onto the chubby haired bodies of buzzing bees. The blaring ensemble of the cicadas is hushed.

Omar booms, "Hey, I'm glad they're gone. That dog never did like me," he says as he grabs his butt and still torn and bloodied pants. "And if yous want, I can get rid of Huxley, too."

Bael and Peter look up but do not say anything.

Huxley's eyes widen, and he crosses his arms and tightly hugs his small body. Omar shrugs. "I'd say suit yourself, but it's not like yous are gonna get dressed up or nothin'."

"Bael," Omar asks, "without Zack around, will yous teach me how to do magic?"

In unison, Bael and Peter say, "NO!"

Omar throws his arms up and then angrily crosses them with his massive biceps flexing like they have a mind of their own—popping like large kernels of popcorn. He starts punching his big fat fist into the palm of his hand and shoots a sideways glance in Peter's direction.

"Huxley," orders Omar, "walk back here with me!"

"Um, o—okay."

"Listen..." but before he can even get his next words out, Huxley hunches down low and throws his arms up and over his head in a defensive position with his little body shaking like a leaf on a tree.

"Wimp! Listen, I want you to talk to Bael."

"About what?"

"I don't care. I just need Petey gone. Got it?" he says as he raises his fist and punches one of his hands against the other right in Huxley's face. Huxley goes cross-eyed as he sees the fist coming closer and closer to him feeling the rush of air, but Omar stops just short of his dripping nose.

Huxley runs up ahead. "Mr.—Mr. Bael, sir. May I—I t—talk to y—you?"

Bael responds, "What is it, Huxley?"

"I w—wondered if you can tell me about—about the..."

"Spit it out, child."

"About the farm."

Meanwhile, Omar whispers, "Sssp...Hey, Peter, come back here for a minute."

Rolling his eyes, Peter asks, "What do you want, Omar?"

"I just thought that it's a nice day out."

"I'm glad you learned how to think."

"And well...isn't it weird you don't hear no birds?"

"You realize that's a double negative."

"Huh?"

Omar chuckles, "But I can show you a bird if you want."

Peter rolls his eyes and yawns. "Clever...but I'm bored." He takes a rushed step forward to catch back up with Bael.

Without those blue eyes fixed on him, Omar reaches into his back pocket and takes out the scrunched-up pillowcase he stole from the hotel. He sneaks up behind Peter and pulls it over his head. Omar lifts Peter off the ground by the head-wrapped pillowcase and brings him several inches off the ground in one swift motion. With the full force of his body weight, he slams Peter to the ground. Something cracks as Peter struggles to break free of the much-heavier Omar.

Omar uses his body weight to pin Peter to the ground. He wraps his thick hands around Peter's neck and squeezes with all his strength. Peter tries to scream out, but his voice is extinguished. He will be, too, if he doesn't get this brute off of him.

Peter's eyes roll back inside his eye sockets. Their beautiful blue power evaporizes. He says an apology to the father he'll never really know.

Bael's eyes flash crimson, and he uses his supernatural speed to appear right before the two boys. Peter had no sooner said his apology when...WHOOSH...Bael was there.

He grabs the hair on the back of Omar's head and flips him with the ease of a pancake. Bael's face lights up with a maniacal smile as he pushes the palm of his hands into the flesh on Omar's chest and leaves his mark as effortlessly as applying pressure to memory foam.

Bael's white-hot hands burn the boy's muscular flesh. When he lifts them, he leaves two large, charred and smoking handprints like the sizzling and burning of flesh left behind from a branding iron. The smell of burnt hair and flesh permeate the air.

Peter yanks the pillow case off of his head and breathes in deeply. Tasting the scent of Omar's flesh—he violently begins spitting, trying to get rid of the taste. Out of breath, Peter says, "UGH! And—I—thought—burnt—popcorn—smelled—bad!"

Omar writhes in pain. He begs and pleads for Bael's forgiveness. Not interested in his blubbering, Bael taunts him like a cat with its prey. Naturally, much like the cat, he has no intention of eating him, but he will give him a slow and agonizing death nonetheless and *enjoy every minute of it.*

"Peter, it's time you practice your fire-starting skills on flesh."

"I tried it on the spiders already."

"Right. Let's see if you can do more than just anger some miniscule ants. Remember, you must stare deeply at him. Take a deep breath. Fill your body with air from your chest to the tips of your fingers and toes. Let your anger take control of you. Pour all your hatred and rage into compelling his flesh to ignite."

"Ugh, but the smell of Eau-de-Omar is in the air!"

"Peter!"

"Okay, okay. I've got this," Peter says as his eyes begin to pulsate like a praying mantis preparing to eat her mate for lunch.

"But before you do, I want Omar to see what's in store for him. If you don't mind, I'd like to give him a sneak peek. Let Huxley watch, too. It will be good for him to know what a cruel death I can inflict upon him should the time warrant it."

"Go for it."

Bael raises his hands and excitedly makes something happen.

"They're coming. Can you hear them, son?"

"It sounds like...like a baby's rattle."

Omar cries, "W—w—what's coming?"

"Patience."

The crackling of dried up leaves on the forest floor begins to get louder and louder. The faint rattling sound gets closer and closer.

"W-w-what...babies? Did...did...you call babies?" asks Omar.

Bael cackles, "You should be so lucky!"

There is movement in the leaves as two eight-foot male rattlesnakes emerge from the darkness. The two snakes keep wrapping themselves around each other as they fight to gain the highest position in front of Bael.

"Easy, my friends. There's enough for both of you."

Bael stares into their eyes. After a long and awkward moment, the snakes bob their heads and slither towards Omar, rattling their tails as they go.

Bael cackles, "Do not give them a reason to bite you, Omar. They will not hesitate to do so. It would give them great joy to sample your flesh!"

They slither their bodies in circles around Omar's feet. With a nod from Bael, they travel up and along Omar's legs only stopping for each to switch position onto the alternating leg. Then it's a race up to his face. The venomous beasts stand again and rattle their tails as though begging like a dog.

Bael gives one nod of his head, and the two hiss and plunge their fangs deep into the side of Omar's neck. Blood lets out like the turning of a faucet. Huxley watches in horror. The snakes' fangs continue to move and pierce his flesh. Once his neck is dotted and swollen like a pufferfish, Bael fixes his gaze upon the serpents.

Suddenly, the tips of their rattles smoke and light on fire. The snakes turn to flee in shock, but Bael sends the fire cascading up their bodies like the fire snake experiment Peter did in science class. Except for the charred remains on top of Omar's torso are from real snakes and not from the chemical reaction of sugar and sulfuric acid.

"Okay, son. Go ahead."

"Quick question first."

"Yes?"

"I thought you said that animals were the exception to your powers."

"Indeed. But what I said is they are generally the exception to my powers. Do you recall what adorns that mirror in your bedroom?"

"Yes, my slobber. I licked it."

"Attractive. Anything else?"

Peter was lost in thought for a split second, and then a smile of remembrance lit his face. Yes. Snakes. Lots of them. Some even had two heads."

"Too right. Snakes, son, are the exception. Now please light this boy up unless you intend to wait and use him like a campfire later on tonight once it's dark. In which case, he'll be much better than those tiny twigs you fetched for me earlier."

Peter chants the directions. Omar's clothes begin to release a deep gray cloud of smoke but quickly extinguish.

"Keep trying, son. We're not in a hurry."

Peter perseveres—starting and stopping the chant a dozen times. On his thirteenth attempt, Omar lights up like the skies on the Fourth of July.

Omar screams, "Huxley, please help me. Please help me. Please..."

Huxley screams in horror, "Stop! Stop! Stop!" but Bael and Peter laugh as they watch. Once he's fully ablaze, his body suddenly transforms into a black-winged bat. He lets out a sharp squeak and flies off into the sky, leaving a trail of smoke in his wake.

Peter says, "Now talk about ashes to ashes."

"Well done, son!"

"Hey, how did you summon the snakes?"

"Snakes are remarkable in the fact that they are just looking for the opportunity to do something that is already in their nature to do. I just provided the incentive and opportunity for them to do it."

"How did you turn him into a bat?"

"You see, son, humans are mindless creatures and incredibly easy to fool. I've seen lesser species with more common sense. Even when presented with the facts, they'd rather believe in a host of urban legends. Some women even go so far as to tie their hair back before going out into the evening to prevent bats from swooping down into their hair and setting up shop. However, in all their bad press, bats serve a vital role in maintaining the very species that wish to eradicate them from the face of the earth. It is this hatred garnered by humans that allows me to transform this power and use it on the object of their hate."

"That's pretty cool. So, following this logic, I hate bees. Can you turn things into a swarm of human-hating buzzers who wield their own built-in swords?"

"That is the general idea, yes."

"And what about mosquitos? I REALLY HATE those little bloodsuckers!"

"What makes you think I don't *already* control them?"

"Well—well, that's not possible. You would have stopped them from sucking my blood."

He raises his eyebrows and smirks. "Would I have?"

Kicking at the earth in front of him, Peter drops his voice and asks, "Why didn't you tell me you were my father?"

"Son, I wanted to. You and I are both dark elves, but you didn't know it yet. I didn't want to scare you by telling you too much, too fast."

"Well, you'll never know how I would have reacted."

"If I told you and you didn't believe me, what would I have done?"

"Do you have any more secrets you're not telling me?"

"Son, dark elves are called that for a reason."

Chapter 18

Zack and Sully had scrambled for the tree line during their frenzied escape. They now wander hopelessly—around—and around—and around. The trees' webbed canopy is tall and dense as they grow in a bidding competition for sunlight, allowing little to permeate down to the forest floor. There's a host of chipmunks and insects scampering around the seemingly endless layer of grass and moss. The plant called *Sweet After Death* litters the forest floor. Zack gulps loudly and hopes that it's not a sign of what's to come.

Out of breath, Zack doubles over. "I—think—we're—going—in—circles."

As if on cue, Sully puts his wet nose on Zack's leg—nudges him—and takes the lead. They trudge up a steep embankment and then back down to a babbling creek. Sully throws himself into the water and begins drinking wildly. So much so that Zack wonders if the creek is babbling or the sound is coming from Sully. The water settles right at the dog's neck, leaving only his eyes and ears visible. Zack chuckles—looks around for any sign of the evil duo—and then back towards Sully. He's gone! *Did he go under? Did the water carry him downstream?*

Zack drops to his knees and screams his name. Tears fall from his bloodshot eyes and run in thick waves down his face. In the blink of an eye, what little he had in this world is now—gone.

In that instant, he mutters, "I don't care if they find me..."

Splash! Gurgle! Splash! Zack looks up. To his amazement, Sully is rolling around in the water like a flounder. No, no, like a sea otter. He goes up—down—up—down. Zack paddles through the water as fast as he can. He snatches up the dog and plants a big kiss right on the dog's wet snout!

"Erruff!"

He puts the dog down and says, "Okay, Sully. It's time to get out of the water."

Splash, gurgle, splash!

"Come on, buddy!"

Blubb, blubb, blubb!

"Hey, do you want a treat?"

Splash, gurgle, splash!

"Okay, I get it. You love the water, but—WE—HAVE—TO—GO—NOW!"

But the dog continues to ignore him and splashes in the water like a two-year-old child in a bathtub. Zack sloshes through the water and scoops up the drenched dog, who is now heavier with added water weight. Wincing, he struggles through the water, trying desperately not to fall and send them both racing downstream. He makes it to the edge and flops the dog down onto the earth with a hearty, wet thud. Sully shakes wildly and sends about three-quarters of the water right onto Zack, who doesn't have the same built-in propensity for ridding his saturated clothing of its water.

As they walk, the trees open up, and smaller and less mature trees have started to take hold. Beautiful wildflowers surround them with fat little bumblebees merrily sipping nectar and flitting about. The wildly growing grass is past Zack's knees, with much of it already going to seed. Sully can't see past the tall grass and resorts to hopping like Tigger from *Winnie the Pooh* just to see what's in front of him.

They continue for just a few minutes when Sully leads them to a clearing. Zack looks up and cups his hands over his eyes to block the brilliant light of the sun as he attempts to study something flying high overhead. It keeps getting lower and lower as it makes several passes over their heads.

The serene landscape is at once ruined when an aggressive black-winged bat swoops down on them and attempts to plant its outstretched claws into Zack's scalp. He screams and protectively throws his arms over his head. The bat makes contact with his arms and scoops out a deep well of blood and skin. Zack cries out and attempts to flee but trips over a rock and lands face-first onto the hard earth. The bat circles back just as Zack rolls over. It's about to claw his eyes out when Sully runs, leaps onto Zack's shoulders, and propels himself into the air. He opens his mouth wide and snatches the bat like a well-placed pitch.

The bat is nestled in the dog's mouth when he quickly spits it out. The bat's wings are wet with the thick, viscous drool and can't fly away. Sully tilts his head to the side. Then to the other side. He bends down and touches his wet nose to the bat. Sniffs. And sneezes wet goo onto the bat.

"Thanks, Sully! You saved me, buddy!"

"Ruff!"

Chuckling, "Yeah, that was pretty rough. But what are you trying to tell me?"

Sully turns his head to the other side, walks over to the bat, and lifts his leg. The bat hops a few inches but is still rendered flightless. The dog drank a lot of water from the babbling stream and proceeds to saturate the bat even more as he relieves himself for what seems like a straight minute. Zack's eyes bulge as he watches what Sully is doing. Too stunned to do anything. Not sure he'd want to anyway. He just watches, enjoying the payback. Once Sully can *go no more*, the two walk away, leaving the bat to air dry.

They end up on a dead-end street where the trees are droopy and look as depressed as Zack feels. One of the large oak trees has a red and white bullseye painted on it with an assortment of paintball splotches outlining it like a color wheel. Worse than the defaced tree is the horrible display of aim—or lack thereof—cast by its defilers. The homes and boarded up with hideous sheets of plywood and leftover scraps of wood. Graffiti litters the homes where *graffiti artists* left their calling cards and various other nonsensical, bulbous-looking illustrations.

Zack sits down on an abandoned doorstep with his wet shoes letting out a sloshing sound. He deposits his sad and defeated face into his dirt-stained hands and shakes his head in disgust.

"I knew better! I knew better! When something seems

too good to be true, guess what, Sully!" he says as he absentmindedly scratches between the dog's ears. "It usually is!"

He wasn't wanted by anyone. And what were Bael's *true intentions* with him anyway? Omar and Huxley knew him the best and *they* didn't want him either. In the end, they turned against him and sided with a stranger. An evil stranger at that!

"Well," he whispers, "that's not entirely true. I have you." He plants another kiss on the dog's forehead and retreats before Sully can return in kind.

Tears roll down Zack's face ridding it of some dirt, when a man in dilapidated old car spies the boy and dog. He slows down. The car makes a series of crude sounds before coming to a stop, leaking something green and noxious from the rear of the vehicle. The door creaks open, and out steps a man with pants that are about six inches too short for his gangly-looking legs. The hair on his face is unkempt and scruffy. His long-sleeved shirt looks more like a three-quarters shirt and ends midway between his elbow and wrist, and reveals the stains of several of his most recent meals. Homemade-looking green tattoos litter his arms like long sleeves.

"Hey, kid. Did you do this?" asks the man pointing at the graffiti.

"No!" says Zack in a snarky voice.

"Then how did it all get there?"

"Do you really think I did this just now? If so, you must be the long-lost father of a boy named Omar."

He turns his head to the side. "Then just what exactly are you doing here then? People don't just come here. I suppose you're going to say that you just stumbled upon it or something."

"I guess I could ask you the same. Based on the colorful stains on your fingertips, I'd bet you have a load of spray-paint in that pathetic car of yours!"

"Why you little punk!" screams the man, and he chases after him.

"RUN, SULLY!"

Zack and Sully run for cover behind a house with an intricately designed red and black dragon. A large pile of ratty old tires and tall grass are the only things separating them from the fast-approaching man. With no place else to go, Peter and Sully leap behind the tires. The man is not fooled and heads straight towards their hiding spot. He brings back his ratty old boot, kicks the base of the pile, and send the tires falling like dominos. Zack throws some tires aside.

They swiftly abandon the backyard and jump a series of small fences like hurdles. If Zack wasn't so scared of being caught, he would have stopped to compliment Sully on his jumping skills. The dog looks like an Olympian as he stretches his back legs in an almost horizontal position as he casts himself through the air.

The gangly man could easily step over the small fences but instead tries to jump them. Lucky for them, his foot catches on a piece of chain-link wire, and he goes down with a thud. They continue to add some space between them and the man when, next, Sully's foot gets caught. The dog whimpers loudly like a mouse caught in a mousetrap. Zack stops dead in his tracks and turns around to help free him when the man catches back up to them.

He roughly grabs Zack by the scruff of his neck and throws him to the ground knocking the wind right out of him. The man pays no attention to Sully, who now anxiously circles the two of them with the hair on his back at full attention. The man straddles Zack's body and plants his knee squarely into his back. He uses his hands to push Zack's head hard into the brown earth. Zack screams out in pain and ingests a mouthful of dirt.

The gangly man says, "Now, you give me one good reason why I shouldn't beat the backtalk out of you right now, you filthy little punk!"

Zack lets out a muffled sound.

"Speak!"

He lets out another unintelligible sound.

The man loosens his grip and slightly lifts his planted knee. Zack turns his head to the side and spits out a mound of earth. "Get—off—of—me!"

Out of breath, the man says, "Now—I'm going to let you up—but—don't even think about running," the man says as he slowly gets up, never taking his eyes off him. "There's no place you can go here that I can't find you."

Just then, Sully, who had stayed quiet until just this moment, lunges at the man and catches him off guard. The man hits the ground with a loud thud and is temporarily unable to move.

"Run, Sully!"

The duo set off at a record-breaking pace before the man even realizes what direction they went in. They continue for several minutes. Zack doubles over—his hands on his knees as his chest heaves up and down. His head throbs with a rush of blood flow. Meanwhile, Sully contentedly performs a series of stretches like he just woke up. He finishes extending his front legs and stretching his hind legs when there's a sound of approaching footsteps.

With his heart now in the pit of his stomach, Zack looks up. But no, it can't be. Sully stops stretching and lets out a low, fierce growl. The hair on his back is up again.

Zack roughly rubs his eyes, then closes them for a few brief seconds, but yet an eternity. He blinks hard. Rubs his eyes again. His body goes limp like a noodle as if already surrendering in defeat.

"I told you that you were bound to me. Did you doubt me you stupid human?" asks Bael.

There they are. Bael stands before him with his menacing eyes fixed on Zack. Peter's eyes glimmer as he rubs his hands together in eager anticipation. Huxley trails behind them. Zack heart beats wildly in the base of his throat, along with the pungent taste of thick bile. At least Omar isn't there—not that it's going to matter anyway. He and Sully are toast!

Bael's face lights up like a crazed madman escaping the confines of a mental hospital. Speaking like he has something bitter and revolting in his mouth, Bael says, "So, we meet again, you stupid, stupid human. I see you still have that mutt with you. Well," he says in a menacing tone, "I can take care of that." A smile spills from his lips.

Bael rounds on Sully and extends his long, bony hand and reaches for the dog's collar. Sully puffs up and stands his ground. His four legs push into the brown earth. His collar begins to emanate brilliant colors and looks almost like it's dancing with Bael's menacing, blue eyes. Bael circles Sully and forces the dog to move in turn, like a well-choreographed dance. Peter and Huxley quietly sit back and watch—both with opposing facial expressions. The two continue to slowly circle each other, creating a trail of rainbow-colored light in their wake.

Bael steps on a twig causing it to snap in two. He momentarily turns his head in the direction of the sound. Zack wastes no time and pounces on Bael's back. The two fall to the ground and begin rolling around for dominance like an alligator's death roll. Bael uses his arms and legs to pin Zack to the ground. His hands fix on both of Zack's shoulders, and they begin to smolder. Zack cries out in pain, breathes hard, and punches his right arm free.

He struggles. Reaches. Just a little more. He pulls something out of his pocket. Its jagged edges carve into Zack's skin. Crimson runs down his hands. Reaching around, he grabs a handful of Bael's strong blond hair.

Bael's head snaps back, and Zack pushes his hand up further and lands on Bael's left eye. He buries his fingers into Bael's eyelid and pries it open, leaving behind four-finger impressions. Simultaneously, Sully faces Peter and Huxley and flashes his bright collar at them, creating a red film of light that engulfs them like a Christmas bulb. Peter pushes his hand forward, but it's stopped when it meets the forcefield.

Peter throws both hands out and touches the forcefield like a maniacal mime. He screams, but Zack can't hear him. He lifts his leg, turns, and does a karate chop. Nothing. Tries again. Nothing. Turning to Huxley, he picks the boy up and hurls him at the barrier. Huxley screams and falls to the ground. They're both trapped. Sully then turns and shoots a flying crimson rope from his collar, and it hogties Bael by all four limbs.

Bael lets out a murderous cry. "Son. Son. You have to help me!"

Zack holds the tiny fragmented mirror in front of Bael's pried-open eye. His face begins to elongate but quickly snaps back into place. Sully turns the light from his collar that's holding off Peter and Huxley and points it at Bael. Bael's face elongates again. His skin ages. His blond hair rapidly turns gray. The crimson rope begins to fall as Bael's aged body shrinks in size. Then suddenly, there's a bright flash of light, and Bael is violently pulled back into the mirror. His skin stretches and pulls away from his body like the fallen skin of a serpent.

For just a moment, none of them can believe what just happened. Sully is the first to react and roughly nudges Zack with his snout. Deep black circles sharply outline Zack's eyes, and a blank look occupies his aged face. His hand absently opens, and he drops the jagged shard of glass onto the ground below. Sully bares his teeth and gently scoops it up. He continues nudging Zack as his limp body just falls forward with each push until he suddenly snaps out of his zombie-like trance. The two turn and run as fast as they can away from Peter and Huxley.

Peter screams, "You can't leave me! You are bound to me!"

Zack screams over his shoulder, "Oh yeah! Just watch me!"

Chapter 19

Huxley's heart beats in his throat—preferring the taste of warm bile over what he fears is about to happen. Would it be better just to let Peter turn him into a bat? To be done with it once and for all? He started ticking off a mental list of what he knew so far. Zack was the only one to get away—albeit bloodied and bruised. He *has* to start thinking like him if he wants to survive.

Peter's skin is pasty white like a ghost. His shimmering blond hair is almost blinding. There seems to be abnormal strength to his locks, too. Peter had food stuck in his teeth one time, and Huxley watched him pluck out a piece of his hair and floss his teeth with it. Perplexed, Huxley tried the same thing, and his hair snapped every single time and only managed to add to what was already stuck.

They can light things on fire. After looking around to make sure he wasn't overheard, Peter had bragged about taunting the ants into fighting. He stopped talking at once when Bael turned up out of seemingly nowhere.

Bael was able to summon rattlesnakes and turned Omar into a bat. And Peter—he called out to Bael without even saying a word. He knew this for sure because he saw Bael's eyes turn crimson when Omar had attacked Peter. Huxley was staring at Bael who was right in front of him, then he wasn't. Did he disappear and reappear in front of Peter? However he did it, Huxley didn't know. His heart races at every turn expecting to see Bael turn up out of nowhere. That was worse than knowing where Bael was. Then he could devise a plan. Now nothing is safe. Nothing is sacred. Nothing.

Peter and Huxley continue to trudge through the woods. It's dusk—the bats will be out soon. Will Omar be among any of them? *And what will he eat? Does he know to sleep upside down? Will he bully the other bats, too?*

Meanwhile, the crickets have started their loud chirps—the males call the females with boisterous songs. Perhaps he will hear a cricket sonnet when two of the insects eagerly find each other. Or do they excitedly break out in song for not falling prey to any of the nocturnal hunters that would like to snack on them as their evening appetizer?

Peter breaks the silence. "Fun fact. Did you know that you can tell the temperature out by the number of times a cricket chirps?"

"H—h—how?" asks Huxley.

Peter shoots an annoying glance at Huxley and rolls his eyes. "You count how many chirps are in one minute, and that will tell you the temperature outside."

Under normal circumstances, Huxley would very much like to test this theory; however, he also very much wants to stay alive. He needs to stay away from Peter's eyes long enough to escape. Maybe he could wait until Peter was distracted by something and run as fast as his legs would take him. No, that wouldn't work—Peter's superhuman speed, or whatever it is, would catch him before he even ran far enough to become winded.

What if he waited until they made it back to the road, and he flagged down a passing car? No, Peter could just set the driver and the vehicle on fire. If he could only find a mirror just like Zack had. Why—oh why—didn't he listen to him? Okay, finding a mirror in the middle of the woods isn't going to happen. But what if any reflective surface would scare Peter off? Like the reflection from water? If Huxley could just find some water, throw himself into it, and manage not to die because he couldn't swim, maybe Peter wouldn't chase him. Just maybe. He shrugged to himself and hung his head low. It's the only plan he can think of. And if he dies, well he will accept that fate, too.

Nightfall is upon them. Without a cloud in the sky, the full moon shines without any obstruction.

"Great," Huxley mumbles to himself, "I'm already with a freak. I don't need to add any werewolves to the mix!"

An owl lurches on a nearby branch looking down with laser-like focus. It swoops down with near-silent flight and uses pinpoint precision to pluck a mouse off the forest floor with its talons. The mouse lets out a shrill scream causing the hair on his arms to stand. What kind of bat is Omar now? Does he prefer fruit—or does he want flesh? Knowing Omar as well as he does, he suspects the latter. He feels as exposed as the mouse.

To his surprise, the moon shines through a break in the trees like a beacon in a storm. He spots a fast-moving stream down beyond a tree-lined embankment. Without the moonlight, he probably would have missed it. He can't even hear it over the sound of the crickets, the snapping twigs below his overly tight shoes that let in water and dirt, and his wildly beating heart. He won't let himself overthink it. He stretches his arms and legs, takes a deep breath, and runs full throttle towards the stream.

His right leg is the first to leap off the ground, quickly followed by his left. In just a split second, he's airborne and flying towards the rushing stream below. Butterflies wildly flutter inside his chest as he does a hard bellyflop into the rushing water below. It's so cold that it cuts right through to his bones. Now floating downstream in the fast-moving water, he angrily smacks off large rocks and tree stumps, struggling to get a mouthful of air before being submerged again into the black of the water. His face tightens as the rushing water inflicts its unforgiving power. Sweeping past bends in the stream and down several small waterfalls, he stops when he smacks hard into a beaver dam. The juxtaposition is not lost on him; where there is violent water on one side, there is peaceful and tranquil water on the other. He coughs several times and spits up mouthfuls of water. Before he can even roll over, he is roughly yanked from the water by the back of his shirt.

Panic fills his eyes as he looks wildly around to see what had grabbed him. Just then, Peter steps out from the shadows. His blue eyes cut through the darkness like a bright flashlight. Huxley falls to all fours and begins to hyperventilate, sending his small frame throbbing up and down in a wild fit.

"You were warned about what would happen if you tried to escape."

With purple lips, he cries, "I—I—I'm s—s—sorry!"

"No, you're not! You're just sorry I caught you. Lucky there was a dam here. Maybe I should keep a beaver as a pet instead of that fleabag dog!"

"F—f—fine i—i—idea."

"The only reason why you're still breathing is that I need you for something."

"W—w—what?"

"We're going to Tom and Kate's house."

"W—w—who's that?"

"Those are the people who stole me from my father and pretended to be my parents."

Hoping to anger Peter enough to put him out of his misery once and for all, Huxley bravely asks, "Aren't you—you m—mad that he didn't tell y—you he is y—your f—father?"

"Listen, Peewee! That *wasn't* his fault. He came back for me. He accepts me for how I am. Don't you think it was hard for him to be stuck in the mirror?"

"W—what d—do you m—mean? St—stuck in a m—mirror?"

"Don't play dumb with me. You saw what Zack and that fleabag did to him. Mirrors are dangerous for us."

"W—w—where d—did Bael go?"

"I'm not sure, but I think he's in a cave. WE are going to get him back—even if YOU have to die in the process. There's a necklace that I need help finding. It belonged to my grandmother."

"What will h—h—happen if we c—c—can't find it?"

"Simple. My use for you will be over, and you will die."

Huxley's eyes enlarge to the size of saucers.

"Get a grip on yourself, Peewee. We need to find a

cop."

"Are y—y—you going to report what happened to Bael?"

"Don't be stupid! No, Huxley, I need the cop for a different reason."

The two begin walking towards the sound of traffic, blowing horns, and squealing tires. A traffic light had malfunctioned, and a police officer is feverishly directing traffic at a four-stop intersection.

"Th—th—there's a c—c—cop," stutters Huxley.

"Don't be stupid, Peewee! Do you think I can just walk up to him while he's directing traffic? Even if he listens to me, he won't be able to help with what I need him to do NOW."

Instead, Peter dons his sad puppy dog eyes—though now blue and not brown—and stops the first woman he encounters. She is walking a long-haired dachshund with pink bows wrapped around her ears and wearing a matching sweater that reads *"Mommy's Girl."*

He clears his throat and says, "Ma'am, I'd like to compliment you on your dog's adorable sweater." "Well, aren't you just a breath of fresh air."

He smiles. "Can you please tell me where I can find the closest police department?"

"Well, honey, are you okay?"

"No, ma'am. I must speak to someone right away." "Say no more. There's an officer that sits in his car just on the other side of the parking lot. He's always watching for people breaking the speed limit. It's just past a small group of trees. Folks can't tell he's there until it's too late. Why then he just tears right off after them and gives out the most traffic tickets in the entire department."

"Thank you, ma'am. Enjoy your walk."

Peter looks at Huxley and flashes his eyes at him. The two boys walk in the direction of the speed trap, hoping to spot the police car.

"We're in luck! There he is. Those nosy old women and their prissy little dogs—they watch *everything!*"

Peter walks up to the police car and looks through the window. The officer inside the car looks like he's in his mid-20s. His babyface is freshly shaven, and his jet-black hair is styled and slicked back—not even a single hair is out of place. A broad smile spreads across his face as he points his radar gun at a passing speeder, pushes his sunglasses up from the bridge of his nose, and turns on his sirens. Peter raps on the window, but the officer doesn't hear him over the siren. He's about to lose his chance when, luckily, the officer looks over at Peter. Peter flashes his eyes at him, and the man turns off his lights and siren. A blank stare takes over his baby face.

The officer hangs his mouth awkwardly open and says, "Yes...". A droplet of spittle glides down his face and lands on the microphone clip attached to his uniform.

Peter says, "Now that's more like it. There's a boy pickpocket who just stole my wallet. He has a dog with him who's part of the scam. The two need to be picked up and brought back to the police department."

"Which—way—is—the—police—department?"

"Dude, seriously! You're the one with the badge. You need to search the tree line on the other side of the park. Say you can help get the boy and his dog to safety. He won't want to listen to you, but say whatever you have to say to get them to the police department. Once he's there, ask him who Peter is. You'll then want to call Peter's parents and give them an update on his last known location. Do you understand me?"

"Yessss."

"Good, now GO!"

"Go where?"

Peter smartly smacks his forehead. "Go find them!"

"At the police department?"

"No! On the other side of the tree line! Do they REALLY trust you with a gun?"

"Do you want me to shoot them?"

Peter turns to Huxley and asks, "Peewee, you try to talk to him!"

Huxley turns to the dazed police officer, "Sir, he—he w—w—wants you to go f—f—find them and bring them to the p—p—police department. Un—un—unharmed."

The officer's face regains its color. He turns to Huxley and asks, "Hey, who are you two?"

Peter says, "Interesting." He flashes his blue eyes again at the officer and drains him of his color. He repeats his original instructions.

Chapter 20

Nearly running their feet over with his car, the police officer takes off in the general direction of where Peter said to find Zack and Sully. He inches past a series of outbuildings used as storage for a menagerie of junk and dump-worthy artifacts. Scanning the tree line, the officer spies something moving off in the distance. He watches and waits. Unsure if it's a person or if his eyes are playing tricks on him. He holds up his radar gun. He aims and clocks movement at three miles per hour, a respectable walking speed. A boy and a dog soon come into focus. He gets out of his car and yells to the boy.

"Hey! Hey, kid!" screams the officer.

Out of breath, Zack huffs, "I—didn't—do—anything—wrong."

"Yeah, yeah. I know. You look like you need some help. Let me take you to the station, and we can figure something out. Besides, it looks like you and your dog could stand something to eat and drink."

The mention of food sends Zack throwing his hands to

his stomach.

"How do I know you're safe? I just got away from a psychopath!"

"That's a shame, kid. Trust me; I'm no psychopath. My name is Officer Davis. Just hop on in, and I'll even let you sit in the front seat with me. You can play with the sirens and the PSA."

"What's a PSA?"

"It's the public address system. It's a megaphone that can project your voice to people outside the car. You'd like it, I promise."

"What about my dog?"

"Do you mind if he hops in the backseat? I really can't have him in the front seat. Police dogs don't even ride up front."

"Can we meet a police dog at the station?"

"Sure! I can call Officer Wally and ask him to bring his dog, Sergeant, to the station and meet us there. He's an intimidating-looking German Shepard. I'll teach you a few of his commands."

"But what if a bad guy yells out a command? Wouldn't the dog listen to him instead?"

"The bad buys would never guess the words. The dogs are trained in a variety of different languages. Somebody would have to study commands in a whole host of languages, and by the time they even got close to figuring out what language the dog knew, Sergeant would already be on top of him."

Zack's shoulders drop, and he leans in towards the officer. He hangs on every word about the police dog.

"Okay, I'll go with you."

"Great! Hop in. Hey, where are your parents? It

doesn't seem safe to have you wandering all over by yourself."

"I don't have any."

"Well, you had parents at one point, but I won't press. Can you tell me then how you got here in the first place?"

Zack turns his head slightly and just stares at him.

"What? Did I say something wrong?"

"No. I'm just surprised you're not pushing me to tell you."

"I'm sure you have your reasons, but I really would like to know how you ended up in this tiny town, though."

"Okay. Well, I met up with a boy named Peter. I'm pretty sure he's a runaway. I saw something on the news before they grabbed the remote control and lobbed it at my head!"

"They?"

"Yeah. He's with this creepy guy named Bael."

"And does this creepy guy have a last name?"

"Uh—I don't know it. That's a good question, though. I'd like to know the answer myself."

"Okay. No problem. Go ahead and hop in."

Zack opens the front door and slowly sits in the passenger seat. The man opens the rear door, and Sully leaps into the car and excitedly runs back and forth on the long leather seat. The car's front panel is loaded with various buttons, a computer, multicolored lights, and complex-looking equipment. Zack quietly looks at the multiple buttons and pushes the one labeled *siren wail*. It immediately triggers a long and continuous screeching sound. Sully starts to bark and Zack turns it off.

Zack asks, "What will happen if I switch it to *siren yelp*?" but doesn't wait for an answer. The sound changes to a faster version of the first sound. Sully howls even louder at the next sound. Zack quickly turns it off and then rolls down the back windows for the Sully. The dog scampers to the open window and hangs his head out. Zack laughs as looks in the rearview window and can see the dog's jowls flapping wildly in the wind.

The officer turns his blinker on and pulls into the Town of Wilton Police Department. "Okay, kid. You just stick with me, and we'll get this whole thing squared away. How about I order us some lunch? What are you in the mood for?"

"I'm not picky. Just *please,* not a cheese sandwich."

"Got it! Okay, let's go in. You can wait in the squad room while I wrangle us up some lunch."

He gestures to a chair and says, "Okay, you can sit right here."

Zack sits down at a coffee-stained desk in the squad room that's overflowing with various pictures of suspects, police reports, and other police-related paraphernalia. He tries to look away from the large stack of mug shots but throws his hands up and walks over to the desk. He looks through about a dozen pictures and lands on one he knows. His mouth drops as he flips it over and reads the name.

"Hey, this guy works at the foster home I was in."

Officer Davis looks at the wanted picture and says, "The man was arrested for breaking into a grocery store and stealing the entire deli case of meats and cheeses."

"Well," says the police officer, "I can say that this is a first for me. What a weird thing to steal."

"I bet the Portly Lady put him up to it."

"The Portly Lady?"

Throwing his hand back, "Don't worry about it. I just recognized him, is all."

"Okay. I'll be back in a few minutes. Will you be okay?"

"Yeah, I'll be fine."

In about twenty minutes, Officer Davis returns with two McDonald's combo meals. He tosses a bag at Zack and says, "Go ahead and eat this. We'll figure out what's going on once you've eaten. I'll be back in a minute."

Officer Davis takes his lunch and goes into an adjacent room and shuts the door. Sully saunters up and nudges it ajar with his nose. Zack can overhear a one-sided phone conversation.

"Sorry, ma'am. I'm Officer Davis from the Wilton Police De—."

"Ma'am? Ma'am? Are you there?"

"Oh, hello sir. I'm Officer Davis from the Wilton Police Department. I found a boy who claims to have been traveling with your son."

Chapter 21

Mr. Powell drops the phone to the floor and the two rush for the door—getting stuck as they both try to leave at the same time. They both back up to let the other one go first. Then both dart forward to try and fit through at the same time. Mrs. Powell's slender bodyframe allows her to pass right under Mr. Powell. She runs for the car. Mr. Powell catches up to her and they both run straight towards the driver's side and smartly bang into each other and fall backward. Mrs. Powell grabs her head and then backs up to allow her husband to drive. She runs around the front of the car and gets into the passenger seat. They both turn to each other—wide eyed and mouths agape.

Mr. Powell looks at his wife. "Do you have the keys?"

She shrieks, "No! No, I don't have them!"

They both flee the car like it's on fire and dart towards the house. They again bang into each other at the back door to the house. This time Mr. Powell takes a step back and allows his wife to enter first. Mrs. Powell scrambles to the laundry room and fetches her purse in its usual resting place. Throwing her hands into her bag, she feels the metallic spikes of her key chain and pulls them out. Blood runs down her hand. Rubbing her fingers together and sniffing them—it's not blood. It's lipstick.

She wipes the viscous substance on the white hand towel and screams, "I have the keys! Let's go!"

They rush to the back door of the kitchen and violently smack into each other again. They each back up, rush to the door, and smack into each other again with a harsh thud. They repeat this again and again. Mrs. Powell tucks her head and determinedly rushes one more time, hitting her husband squarely in the chest. This time she exits the house and runs to the car, Mr. Powell in hot pursuit behind her. They each take their position in the vehicle.

Mr. Powell shoves the keys into the ignition. He takes the car out of park and puts the pedal to the floor. The wheels begin to squeal, and the smell of burnt rubber permeates the air. Mrs. Powell screams as they rush forward. The car hits the stone archway, and several stones crash to the ground. Without surveying the damage, he slams the car into reverse. The car speeds down the driveway, mangling the yellow rose bush in his wake and then comes to another squealing halt. As if on cue, the nosy neighbor is at the base of the drive walking her prissy dog, Miss Darcy, who today is wearing a bedazzled red dress with sparkling sequins complemented by a white tutu.

"Hey!" screams the nosy neighbor. "No wonder why that kid of yours left with that man!"

Mr. Powell slams on the brakes, causing their necks to snap forward and back violently. He turns to his wife and asks, "What did she just say?"

She says, "She said something about a kid and a man..." She jumps out of her car before her husband even has the door open. She dashes over to the woman and pleads, "What did you say?"

Indignantly, she says, "I screamed, HEY! You almost hit me...AGAIN!"

"Please, please! Did you say something about our son?"

"Oh, him. Why, yes."

Mr. Powell now turns on her. Gritting his teeth, he demands, "If you know what's good for you, you'll tell us right now what you saw!"

The nosy neighbor throws her free hand to her hips. Miss Darcy lets out a low growl. "I saw him, and that unleashed dog leave your house and head off into the woods."

Hot tears of anger stream down Mrs. Powell's face. Through gritted teeth, she seethes, "Why, didn't you tell us? You walk up and down this street all day and all night. You SAW our missing child posters! Why? You know, you truly are a VILE human being!"

She replies, *"I know what he is.* I—know—what—you—protect. Or what you *should have* protected. It's going to happen again. This is all YOUR FAULT!"

Mrs. Powell cries, "I tried. I tried. I—." But that's all she gets out before collapsing on the ground. Mr. Powell gently lifts his wife and brushes off the dirt from her hands and knees.

He says soothingly, "Honey, let's go. Let's see what the police know." He opens her car door and helps her in. He gets into the driver's seat and squeals the car's tires as they head towards the Wilton Police Department.

Mrs. Powell absently stares out the car window. Tears stream down her face and into her open mouth. She mumbles, "Look at all these people. They're just living their lives like nothing is wrong. Like they didn't fail the— fail the—fail—."

He responds, "I know what you're saying. It's like the world has just stopped—like someone punched me with the strength of a gorilla right in the chest. But at the same time, it feels like the world is speeding up. It makes no sense at all. It's just so, so surreal."

They continue looking at the world around them as they pull into the Wilton Police Department's parking lot. They park the car and dash for the glass double doors only to come to a complete halt outside the doors.

"Tom, what are we going to do if we see him?"

"Peter?

"No, you know—."

"I've been wondering that myself."

"He..."

"I know."

"And you..."

"Yes."

Mr. Powell diverts his eyes from her. He reaches forward and opens the heavy glass door. He lightly places his hand on her back, and they both pass through the entrance. Once on the other side, they both protectively grasp each other's sweaty hands. The door closes with a soft whooshing sound behind them—the sound of their sealed fates. But the front desk is empty.

They look down the hallway. There's a long row of benches on either side of the scuffed-up white wall. A young boy is sitting there. He looks to be around Peter's age, and he has Sully with him.

Mrs. Powell lets out another agonizing cry, "Listen. *Whoever—whoever—whoever* that boy is," she says with a quiver to her soft voice, "he has—he has Sully. He must know where Peter is. Peter—would never—ever—have left Sully."

Like an expert swimmer, she uses her hands to push off of Mr. Powell and propel herself down the hallway.

Sully spots them, lets out an excited bark, and runs to them. At the same time, the Powells run to him at full force. They all collide with each other in a rush of excitement, sending all three to the gray tiled floor. Legs and arms wrap around each other lovingly, albeit like a pretzel.

Mrs. Powell rolls over, looks up, and asks pleadingly, "Where is our son?"

"He's with Bael, Omar, and Huxley," Zack says.

The Powells turn to each other. "Who's Omar and Huxley?" they both cry out in unison.

"Bael kind of—uh—adopted us from the—uh—the foster home."

"Foster home? Adopted?" rings out Mrs. Powell. "Doesn't he want to come home?"

"Umm—well—I—umm."

Mr. Powell stops Zack's awkward musings. "You just said it all without really saying it."

Zack stutters, not sure what to say.

Mr. Powell says, "I get it. He never bonded with us. It didn't matter what we did—he always resented us for it. We either loved him *too much* or *not enough*. He always had this—sort of—smoldering hatred for us."

"Yes, Tom. He—he really," Mrs. Powell sniffs deeply, "really did."

Zack listens as they commiserate how much Peter dislikes them. Even as a baby, they couldn't comfort him—couldn't soothe him. Sadly—his first smile was when Mrs. Powell's parents died. Her mother died first—marking Peter's first smile. They attributed this as a coincidence. However, when her father died just two weeks later, marking his second smile—they worried. Would he turn out to be like *him*?

"Excuse me?" says Zack.

"Yes, dear?" answers Mrs. Powell.

"Who were you talking about back there?" Zack asks as he points in the direction of the door.

"It's something we have tried hard to put behind us. Our family—my bloodline," says Mrs. Powell, "has a dark past. We thought we could put an end to it, but I fear we were dreadfully wrong. But please, I must know. Describe this *Bael* person to me."

"Well—he's creepy. I was surprised he wasn't Peter's real dad because the two look so much alike." Noticing their discomfort, he says, "I'm sorry. I just meant that..."

The Powells look at each other with pain in their eyes. "We understand. Truly—we do." With the sound of thirteen years of pent-up pain spilling out, "Please continue."

Clearing his throat, "Well—his eyes—they sort of change."

"Change—change how?"

"Well, they are ice blue, but pulsate with a more intense shade of blue when—when..."

"Yes," motioning with their hands for him to continue.

"This just sounds—well, it sounds stupid."

Cupping her comforting hands over his, "We understand far more than you realize."

He looks up and into her loving eyes. "Can you both excuse me for a minute?" asks Zack.

"Of course, Zack," they reply in unison.

Zack leaves the police department and spots some wildflowers growing across the street. Sully is making loud clicking sounds as he scratches and the glass door to go outside with him, but Zack doesn't turn around. Instead, he carefully selects flowers of every color. Pausing to take the string out from his hoodie—he carefully ties it around the flowers and returns to the police department. Bending on his knees, he presents Mrs. Powell with the flowers. Her forehead wrinkles. Her eyes close. Her cheeks tighten. She sobs so profoundly her chest heaves up and down like she just pushed past the finish ribbon of a marathon.

"I'm so sorry!" Zack quickly exclaims. "Did I offend you?"

"Offend me? Absolutely not! Zack," HONK! "you have so little in this world, yet you're thinking about me!"

Mr. Powell asks Zack, "Are you hungry? Maybe we can all go out for dinner."

Zack responds, "Umm, yeah. That would be great!"

Mr. Powell says, "Excuse me for just a minute. I'm going to find someone to see if we can go next door to the Cracker Barrel. It's just across the street. They can still see us from over here. Is that restaurant okay, Zack?"

"It sure is."

The front desk officer returns. A look of unwavering seriousness displayed on his face.

Mr. Powell gulps loudly and asks permission to take Zack out for dinner.

The officer says, "I'm not sure. Where do you plan on going?"

Mr. Powell answers, "Just right next door," he says as he points to the Cracker Barrel restaurant.

The officer says, "Well, that will save me from having to scrounge up something for him to eat. So, sure. Go ahead, but stay within sight of the police station."

The foursome excuse themselves and walk across the street to the restaurant.

"Those chairs look so comfortable out front," says Zack.

"They are. They're called Adirondack chairs. There's also a neat little shop you pass through on your way to the restaurant," says Mrs. Powell.

"Would you like to take me on in a friendly game of Tic-Tac-Toe?" asks Mr. Powell. "Before you answer, I have to tell you that I'm somewhat of a legend."

"Bring it on!" chuckles Zack.

Mrs. Powell sits back and rocks in one of the rocking chairs, fully absorbing the breathtaking scene unfolding in front of her.

Zack can't explain it, but the more they talk, the more comfortable he feels with them. He can't help but notice the discrepancy between what Peter had said about them and what he now sees for himself.

"Mr. Powell, I'm sorry that Peter doesn't appreciate you. I would give *anything* to have my parents back."

"Thank you, Zack. I won't put you in the middle of it because that wouldn't be fair to you, but I know that he spoke poorly of us. He does the same thing at school, too."

"Yet, you both still want him back?"

"Yes."

"Why?"

"We take our responsibilities seriously. No matter what. And I don't want to pry, but if you want to talk about your parents, we're here for you."

"I—um..."

"Powell Party," bellows the woman on the intercom, "table of 3 is ready."

Sully looks up, "Errrough!"

Mrs. Powell kneels so she's eye-level with the pooch and looks at him. "You can stay quietly under the table, and whatever falls on the floor is yours."

"Huhh, huhh, huhh!" pants Sully as he excitedly runs circles around her.

They enter the restaurant. There are little games at the tables inside, too. One is supposed to test the player's IQ. It's a triangular-shaped peg game where the player has to jump the pegs and however many are left at the end reveals the player's IQ. The fewer the better.

Mrs. Powell snorts as the game reveals that she is an "EG-NO-RA-MOOSE!" Mr. Powell is "JUST PLAIN DUMB!"

"Come on, Zack! You have to try!" they both excitedly urge him on.

He grabs the game, sticks his tongue out to the side, and begins moving the pegs. He continues until there is only one peg left. He did it!

"WOAH!" screams Mr. Powell. "I've been coming to this restaurant since I was a kid, and I've never gotten past being "JUST PLAIN DUMB! Nice job!"

Sully jumps up under the guise of congratulating Zack,

and skillfully grabs one of his mozzarella sticks and crawls back under the table causing them all to have a hearty laugh.

Their dishes had long since been cleared. They continue to joke and laugh like they've always known each other, without a single moment of awkward silence spilling out like he had with Bael. He loves how happy and relaxed Sully is. The silly dog is sound asleep on the floor, propped up by the base of the table, with all four of his own legs dangling up in different directions.

Chapter 22

Peter barks, "Look, freshling, we are in a hurry. I need to try something, but I've never done it before by myself."

Huxley fearfully looks up and asks, "W—w—what?"

Peter blows a puff of air out of his mouth and snatches Huxley's hand, gripping it fiercely. Huxley whimpers out in pain. A few short seconds go by, and the two stop dead in their tracks. They smack squarely into a huge tree with massive roots. Huxley falls to one side, Peter to the other. Huxley rolls over to all fours. Peter quickly moves away from Huxley as fierce retching sounds begin. Huxley's small frame begins dry heaving from his stomach to his toes—unable to vomit because he hasn't consumed any food or water.

Peter screams, "Suck it up, buttercup! We don't have much time!"

As soon as Huxley's dry heaving subsides, Peter grabs his hand again. "Good, there's nothing in you to throw up. Let's go."

They continue with Peter's superhuman speed and arrive at the Powell Family Home. Peter spies the nosy neighbor walking her ankle-biting dog, Miss Darcy. He grabs Huxley's wrist again, and he lets out another whimper. They dart between the woman and her dog, ruffling her long house dress as they pass.

The hair on Miss Darcy's back stands up, and she begins to growl. Peter grabs the woman's wig. She throws both hands to her bare head and absently drops Miss Darcy's leash.

"W—who's there?" she whispers, as she swings her face back and forth, her flapping jowls falling in sync with her movements.

Peter was well past her, but can hear her call out and turns back around—still dragging Huxley in tow. He grabs the bottom of her long dress with his free hand and pulls it up over her head. She screams and attempts to run away but falls to the ground with a thud. Spooked and unrestrained, the dog runs away from her with its tail between its legs, the leash flapping wildly behind it.

"MISS DARCY! MISS DARCY, COME BACK!"

Looking like a drunken blimp of a figure, she falls to her knees, lifts one leg, plants her foot, her butt extends upward, and she raises her other leg. She wobbles in her oversize orthopedic shoes and does a sharp face-plant back down on the sidewalk. She cries out as her glasses break.

Peter giggles and drags Huxley to the family's home. He turns the rear kitchen door, and it opens.

"Great! I don't have to climb through the window."

The lights are still on. The television is blaring. The iron is still plugged in. It's standing up and letting off steady puffs of steam. Peter walks over and pushes it face-down. He chuckles to himself, "An easy alternative to my firepower." He turns to Huxley and flashes his eyes.

"Listen, we need to find a necklace. It's hidden somewhere in this house. We need to check room by room for it. There are lots of hiding places here. Dump drawers out, push things over, do whatever you have to do. We have to find it! Do you understand me?"

With a blank expression, "Yes..."

"You look downstairs. I'm going upstairs. DON'T you dare disappoint me!"

"Yes..."

Peter takes the steps two at a time. He goes to his old bedroom first. The mirror is gone. He walks into his father's study and pulls out his prized first edition books from the shelves, and throws them to the floor. He carefully feels all around the bookshelf for a secret compartment. Throwing the desk open, he tosses out the file folders, gets on his hands and knees, and feels around the baseboards for a button. Something. Anything. Throwing his arms up, he storms out of the room.

His next stop is their bedroom. He looks in the easy spots first, like their dressers and under their bed, tossing the contents onto the floor like a Tasmanian devil. He puts his back up to a tall chest of drawers. It's too tall for his mother. She could never reach the top and always had to fetch a ladder if she wanted to use it. Walking to the side of it, he gives it a smart push. It moves, revealing a set of stairs behind it.

"Bingo!" He runs up the stairs and feels for a light. He looks around and sees the mirror that had brought his biological father back to him. There were impressive family portraits for each of his relatives that had lived in the old house. Looking carefully at each portrait—his mouth falls open. A dog that looks remarkably like Sully is in EVERY portrait.

He squints and says, "And that dog is wearing the same stupid collar in every—single—one! Yup, that's Sully! I'm sure of it! I'd recognize those stupid snaggle teeth anywhere."

Meanwhile, downstairs Huxley looks on the belly of the table, inside the cabinets, and behind the refrigerator and stove. He walks into an adjoining room that contains the washer and dryer. He taps on the walls but notices no discrepant sounds. He wanders out of the room, back through the kitchen, and into the living room. The room has an oversized couch, a love seat, and a reclining chair.

There are large vases with beautiful artificial yellow roses. Huxley is drawn to the roses like a drunken bee. He touches the vase slightly, and it reveals a hidden compartment. It opens through the back and had been perfectly camouflaged. He would never have guessed it was there if he didn't see it open himself. He looks over his shoulder, puts his hand inside, and feels around. Pulling out something cold and metallic, he looks in his hand. He's holding a beautiful, ornate necklace. He's never seen something so beautiful, even from the Portly Lady's collection. She always wore the finest clothing and accessories.

The necklace lights up, and he feels a jolt. He suddenly looks around and feels awake, no longer in a daze. A moment of panic and excitement overcomes him. He stands perfectly still and hears Peter causing chaos upstairs.

"Well, Huxley, this is your time!"

He tiptoes to the back door and winces as the door squeaks as he opens it. He runs down the driveway. Unsure of which way to go, he turns left and runs towards more houses. He notices the nosy neighbor outside, still looking for her dog. He passes by her and continues fleeing. He runs for a couple of blocks when he spies a police officer.

"HELP! HELP!" he screams.

The police vehicle is an SUV with K9 printed in bold letters on each side. He pulls over and comes to a stop. The officer gets out. There is a huge police dog in the rear of the SUV, watching quietly with its steely and intense dark eyes that look almost black.

The officer asks, "What seems to be the problem, buddy?"

"Th—th—this guy named B—B—Bael said he w—w—wanted to adopt three b—b—boys for his f—f—farm. He brought another b—b—boy with him named P—P—Peter and his d—d—dog, S—S—Sully."

At the mention of the dog's name, the police officer tilts his head. "That's a different kind of name for a dog. Continue."

"W—w—well, B—B—Bael turned out to be w—w—worse than the foster home st—st—staff. He—he—he hurts p—p—people. D—d—does stuff with his mind. He—he—he set huge snakes l—l—loose on Omar."

At the revelation of the last detail, Huxley's face goes white; he begins to totter back and forth, then faints. Officer Wally catches him just in time before he hits the hard pavement. He scoops up the frail child and places him in the back seat of the vehicle. The police dog watches through the steel divider and lets out a sad whimper for the child.

Officer Wally radios dispatch, "This is Officer Wally. Be advised that I have a 10-45B. I'm taking a minor child to Wilton General Hospital. Requesting a follow-up with Social Services."

The radio squeaks back, "Copy that, Officer Wally."

The police officer turns on his sirens and speeds off to the Wilton General Hospital. Anxious drivers pull over their vehicles and roll their eyes up in relief as the police officer zips right past them. They arrive at the hospital in just under five minutes. He pulls the car into the emergency room bay, and two nurses rush out to the car with a rolling stretcher. They carefully take Huxley from the rear seat and place him onto the stretcher. Another nurse approaches Officer Wally.

The petite nurse wearing pink scrubs and donning a no-nonsense look and asks, "Officer Wally, what can you tell me?"

"Poor fellow passed out. Lucky I caught him."

"Okay. Look, can you stick around and talk to Social Services when they arrive?"

"I sure can. Do you have any of those homemade powdered donuts in the break room still?"

She smiles and says, "Yes, Sharon just made a fresh batch this morning."

"Copy that. You'll know where to find me then?"

She winks and says, "Yes, I'll send Social Services to you there. Just be sure to wipe the powder from your mouth this time."

Pink colors his face as he replies, "Copy that."

He turns and heads towards the break room, his nose

leading the way. He opens the door and saunters over to the fresh platter of donuts. He turns his mouth down as he pours a cup of coffee. He dips his donut into his coffee and brings the gooey mess to his mouth. Some coffee drips down his face, leaving some powder behind. The door opens, and in walks a stern-faced social worker.

He says with a mouthful, "That didn't take long."

She is wearing a gray tweed jacket and ankle-length matching skirt. Her gray hair is pulled back tightly into a bun, causing her wrinkled face to smooth at her hairline.

Looking scornfully at Officer Wally, "Attractive. Please do finish chewing first, Officer. But kindly hurry. My caseload is not getting any smaller thanks to you."

Smack, smack, smack. Gulp, gulp, gulp. Swallow. "Sorry about that. I was on my way back to the station when this boy flagged me down. He..."

"Yes, I already read what the nurse wrote down. I want to know why this kid is my problem."

"Always a gem, aren't you, Ms. Grumpy Pants! Well, the boy needs to go somewhere once he's discharged. He was taken from The Amsterdam Foster Home by..."

"Perfect! That's in Montgomery County. This is Saratoga County..."

"Yes, I know what county we're in."

"Well, I'll just contact Montgomery County and have them fetch the boy once he's discharged."

She asks no further questions, turns sharply around on her penny loafers, and marches out of the break room door. Before the door even closes, she has her cell phone out from oversize handbag and has dialed the Montgomery County Department of Social Services' speed dial number.

"Yes, you've landed a new case. Come pick the kid up at the Wilton General Hospital. I understand, but this is your case. I'm hanging up now."

Meanwhile, Huxley is lying on a hospital bed—grossly dehydrated and receiving fluids intravenously. A petite doctor walks into his room.

"I'm Dr. Jacobs, but you can call me Tara. Pulling back his eyelids, she shines a bright light directly into his eyes. He flinches but doesn't pull away. She wraps her thumb and pinky around his wrists with room to overlap her fingers again, vigorously shaking her head. Next, she pinches his arm. The skin is pallid and slow to regain its shape.

"You're severely dehydrated, child. When is the last time you ate or drank?"

"Thr—thr—three days ago."

"When is the last time you've seen a doctor?"

"W—w—when I lived with my grandparents."

"When was that?"

"I—I—I think when I was four or five."

Just then, there's a demanding knock on the hospital room door. Without waiting for an invitation, the door opens, and another social worker enters his room. She is busy on her cell phone, and the doctor shoots her an evil glare.

The young social worker hangs up her cell phone after barking a few commands and says, "I'm here for the kid. I've already called The Amsterdam Foster Home. The caretaker, Claudia, is ready to receive him."

Astounded, the doctor replies, "Receive him! He's not a bag of groceries. He's not going anywhere. This boy needs medical attention."

"Yeah, well, transfer him to the Montgomery County

Hospital. I don't care what you do but do it now. I'm not driving all the way out here again. It's ridicilious I had to do it this time."

"I don't take orders from the likes of YOU. Now get out of MY hospital!"

"Fine! Happy to! The kid is your problem then. Just sign right here."

The social worker pushes a sheet of paper in front of the doctor's nose.

Snatching it and pulling it away from her face, Dr. Bell scoffs, "Gladly!"

The door slams with a thud. "D—d—did I do something wrong?"

"No child, you did not. I don't want you to worry about anything. I'm going to take excellent care of you. Now, what would you like for lunch and dinner today?"

"A—a—anything."

"Well, you must have some favorites."

Hanging his head low, he mutters, "A—a—at the foster home, I—I—I ate from—from—from the g—g—garbage can."

"YOU WHAT! That does it! I know you don't know me, but when you feel better, would you like to stay with me at my house until we can figure out a better plan for you?"

"W—w—why would you do that?"

Now it's her turn to hang her head. "My son has just gone off to college. His father died five years ago. The truth is," hanging her head, "the house is big, and I am quite lonely."

A pained smile creases Huxley's face. "O—o—okay. I—I—I can c—c—cook and c—c—clean for y—y—you."

"You'll do no such thing."

Chapter 23

A t the police department, Mr. and Mrs. Powell gently ask Zack to sit with Sully while they talk privately for a moment.

"Yeah, sure," agrees Zack. Mrs. Powell motions to the wooden bench right beside her. Zack sits on the bench and calls Sully over to him. The goofy boxer jumps right onto the bench just like a person.

The Powells walk to a nearby room and shut the door. Zack can't hear them but can see them through the glass window. They were deep in conversation—their mouths moving fast. Then the tears came from both of them. She puts her head on his shoulder. He wraps his arm protectively around her.

As Sully and Zack sit there on the uncomfortable wooden bench, he rethinks the conversation he had with the Powells. They care enough about his feelings to ask him to sit there with Sully rather than just telling him to do it. *Has anyone ever made this simple, kind gesture in the past? Like he meant something?* The foster home workers never asked him anything. He was always just told what to do. The other foster kids didn't ask if he was done with something before taking it. They just took it. There was nothing in his life that was simply his. On the rare occasion that he went to a doctor, he wasn't even asked how he felt. The doctors always looked right past him and addressed all their questions to the foster home workers. Like they could accurately describe how HE was feeling!

Zack absentmindedly scratches Sully between the ears. "Well—it looks like I'm all alone again. This hurts more than it did just a week ago." Was knowing what he was missing better than not knowing at all? He didn't think so.

Zack knows the police will return him straight away to the foster home, and the Powells will take Sully back home with them. With tears in his eyes, Zack turns to Sully.

"Well, buddy, it looks like you'll be going back home soon. I'll miss you, but I'm happy that you'll be with your family again. A proper family."

Although the thought of losing Sully devastates him, he can't escape the loving feeling that emanates from the Powells. He tries to distance himself from this thought. But he can't shake the idea that they look at him—actually look AT HIM. Sure, Zack had had plenty of conversations with other adults, but he never felt like they listened to him. The Powells are different.

"Buddy—you are going to have to go soon." Through his tears, he says, "I want you to know that you should go with them. They're your family. I will always—always love you!"

Sully shakes his head violently, sending his jowls flying back and forth. They both look up when they hear the

Powells return. Mr. and Mrs. Powell each take a seat on the bench on either side of Zack.

"Zack," says Mr. Powell, "we both talked it over." Since you don't have a family, would you like to come and live with us? To be our son *forever*? But of course, we understand if you don't want to. But if you do..."

Before Mr. Powell could even finish his thought, Zack turns from side to side, looking at the Powells, and blurts out, "Of course I do! Yes, I want to live with you! Yes, I want to be your son! Yes!"

Just as suddenly, a wave of panic rushes through Zack. It couldn't be that easy. Why did he make himself look so desperate by agreeing so fast? *"There I go again, just opening myself up."*

Mrs. Powell begins to explain, "First, we have to go to court and ask the judge for permission for you to live with us. It's the judge's job to make sure that you'd be safe living with us. In the meantime, they have a place for you to stay until the judge makes her decision. She will also want to talk to you. Is all of that okay with you?"

"Yes, but you seem to know an awful lot about this kind of stuff," says Zack.

Mrs. Powell responds, "Yes, I do, Zack. I sure do."

She continues to explain the process. Zack tries to calm his beating heart by assuring himself that this won't happen and not get too excited. Something will surely go wrong. *But just what if?*

With that, Zack can't contain his excitement and again yells loudly, "Yes, yes! That's all okay! I'll talk to anyone. I'll stay anywhere until I can go home with you! Anything! Just anything!"

Chapter 24

The Powells arrive at the court building an hour early. They anxiously pace up and down the courthouse hall as they wait to be called by Judge Crossly.

"I don't know," whispers Mr. Powell, "this judge has a reputation of making up her mind before she hears all the facts. I just hope she listens to us."

Just then, Principal Payne, the school secretary, and Mr. Johnson walk into the court building.

Mrs. Powell incredulously looks at her husband. "What are THEY doing here? Do you think they're here because of *us*?"

The door opens, and the Powells' name is called. They didn't have to wonder for very long because the principal, secretary, and Mr. Johnson follow them into the courtroom. The Powells mistakenly sit on the wrong side of the room.

"No," the bailiff says rudely, "you sit over there" as he points to a table directly across from where they are sitting. They both gulp with fear.

As her first order of business, Judge Crossly calls Mrs. Powell to the stand.

"Ms. Powell, is it your intention to request to adopt minor child Zacharias Griffin?"

Meekly responding to the judge, "Y—y—yes, your honor. Yes, it is."

"Well, do you understand that I must first judge whether or not this would be a safe placement for Zacharias?" Mrs. Powell nods her in understanding.

"Mrs. Powell, let's first assess your insight as a parent."

"Y—yes, your honor."

"Who was responsible for keeping that evil mirror at your home?"

"I—i—it was me, your honor."

"I see. And you left it where your natural son had access to it?"

"Yes, but..."

"Ms. Powell, a simple yes or no will suffice."

"But you said *natural* son. We adopted him when he was just an infant. He's still our son, but not our natural son. We never told him."

"Thank you for that sidebar comment, but you are his legal parents, and he went missing under your care. Is that correct?"

"Well, yes."

"And now you want to adopt another child?"

"Yes, but..."

"Despite that, you still think that it's safe for Zacharias to be in your care?"

"Yes, because..."

"Well, I have asked Principal Moody to testify as to your fitness as a parent. Please go take a seat and let's hear what she has to say."

Mrs. Powell stands up. Her legs are wobbly. She holds on to the witness box banister as she places one foot in front of the other. She slowly returns to the table where Mr. Powell is sitting. He buries his face in his aged hands.

Principal Payne stands up with her hair and outfit perfectly coifed. She takes the stand, and it seems like there's an entirely new judge asking the questions.

Facing the principal, "Ma'am, can you please tell me what your experience was like with Ms. Powell?"

In a righteous tone, "I certainly can! Ms. Powell has been one of the most irresponsible and neglectful parents that I have had the misfortune of working with in over 20 years in education."

The judge asks, "Is that so?"

"It certainly is! She even told me on one occasion that she knew that it was an inconvenience for her child's teacher every time she arrived late, but she still could not be bothered to get that child to school on time! And then, if you will, the child went missing! Our school and its students continue to be devastated!" As if on cue, the school secretary loudly blows her nose and wipes away her tears.

Mr. Johnson interrupts the momentary lapse in testimony and bellows out, "That woman has no respect for the law!"

Judge Crossly turns towards Mrs. Powell with disgust on her face. "Tell me, Principal Payne, do you feel like another child would be well-cared for in the Powells' home?"

"ABSOLUTELY NOT!"

"Thank you, Principal Payne; I think I've heard all that I need to hear."

"Mr. and Ms. Powell, I have made my decision. You are not fit parents for Zacharias. Understand that this court will not change its decision *unless and until* there is compelling evidence to suggest that you two are fit parents. As it stands, you are not even fit parents to your own child." With a pounding of the gavel, Judge Crossly leaves the courtroom and a stunned Mr. and Mrs. Powell.

Mr. Powell looks at his wife. "How are we ever going to tell Zack?"

As they leave the courtroom, they see Zack darting away from the social worker sitting with him. His look of anticipation and joy changes back to his lifetime experience of grief and sadness.

"That's okay; you don't have to say anything."

Chapter 25

Zack sits at the train station with Mr. and Mrs. Powell and Sully as they wait for the train.

"Zack," whispers Mrs. Powell as she takes his hand in hers, "we wish you could have stayed with us."

Fighting back the tears in his eyes, he looks up and says, "I know."

"We also know how much you love Sully."

Talking over each other, Mr. and Mrs. Powell excitedly blurt out, "You can take Sully with you! He can be yours forever!"

Zack stutters, "That's kind of you, b—b—but I'm going back to the foster home. I'm not allowed to have a dog there."

"You're right," says Mrs. Powell, who isn't trying to fight back the tears, "no dogs *were* allowed there. However, the group home director, Miss Claudia, was fond of Sully when she met him before. That, along with a nice donation, and she said that as long as you agree to take care of him, that he can go with you."

"I agree, I agree!" Zack promises. "But how am I going to get him there?"

Mr. Powell takes two tickets out of his pocket. "One ticket is for you, son, and the other ticket is for Sully. You can both be in the same private car together."

"Mr. Powell, you called me son. I'm not your son. The court wouldn't let you adopt me."

Mr. Powell sternly looks at Zack, "Son, the court can tell us that you can't live with us for *now,* but they can't tell us who we can love or who we can make a part of our family. THAT, my son, is for us to decide together. Although we might be separated *for now*, you and Sully will come back home to us one day. We just don't know yet when that will be. We'll visit as much as we possibly can." As though on cue, Sully licks Mr. Powell's face from chin to forehead with one long swipe of his tongue.

Zack purses his lips together, trying to think of something, anything, to say to break the tension of the moment. "Do you want to keep Sully's dog tag to remember him by?" Zack reaches down and looks closely at the silver tag attached to the dog's collar for the first time.

Mrs. Powell looks at her husband and says, "I think it's time."

"I quite agree, dear."

She bends down and gives Sully a gentle scratch between the ears. She grasps the tag and fondly rubs the raised font. "Sully is short for Sultan, which means one who has magic powers."

"So, you mean...?"

"Yes."

Just then, the conductor makes the final boarding call.

The Powells hold hands as they watch Zack and Sully board the train. Zack reaches into his pockets for the train tickets. What's this? He pulls out the mirror that he used to capture Bael. Sully turns his head to the side.

"Sully—why do I get the feeling that there's more to this story?"

About Atmosphere Press

Atmosphere Press is an independent, full-service publisher for excellent books in all genres and for all audiences. Learn more about what we do at atmospherepress.com.

We encourage you to check out some of Atmosphere's latest releases, which are available at Amazon.com and via order from your local bookstore:

Saints and Martyrs: A Novel, by Aaron Roe

When I Am Ashes, a novel by Amber Rose

Melancholy Vision: A Revolution Series Novel, by L.C. Hamilton

The Recoleta Stories, by Bryon Esmond Butler

Voodoo Hideaway, a novel by Vance Cariaga

Hart Street and Main, a novel by Tabitha Sprunger

The Weed Lady, a novel by Shea R. Embry

A Book of Life, a novel by David Ellis

It Was Called a Home, a novel by Brian Nisun

Grace, a novel by Nancy Allen

Shifted, a novel by KristaLyn A. Vetovich

Because the Sky is a Thousand Soft Hurts, stories by Elizabeth Kirschner

About the Author

Theresa is a veteran educator and teaches an exceptional group of military-connected students. She recently moved from Japan to Kentucky with her faithful rescue dog, Sadie Mae.

In her free time, Theresa likes to be taken on long walks by her dog (yes, the dog is in charge), is an avid reader and writer of middle-grade fiction, and enjoys planning creative activities for her students. Her classroom has been vandalized by naughty leprechauns who thwart would-be treasure hunters and deposit tiny *nuggets* behind—and gingerbread cookies who run rampant throughout the school, teasing students with a meager trail of crumbs and notes.

She is amazed at how quickly her students perform *just about anything* with the slightest melody from her angelic voice. The Fat Lady from *Harry Potter* has nothing on her! Perhaps someone should tell her to replicate this behavior training with her dog. This brings us to another point. She often thinks she's funny, even if she's the only one in the room laughing.

Theresa is a passionate supporter of animal rights, and her writing usually includes animal protagonists. Her inspiration is a blend of her previous experience as a Social Worker combined with her classroom experiences—sprinkled with humor and twisted with dark, magical fantasy.

She received a Psychology Degree from the University at Albany, a Master's Degree in Education from East Carolina University, and a Ph.D. in Education from North Central University.

Want to connect more with her? Follow her adventures on Facebook, Instagram, and visit her website at theresanellis.com.

THERESANELLIS